New Adventures of Alice

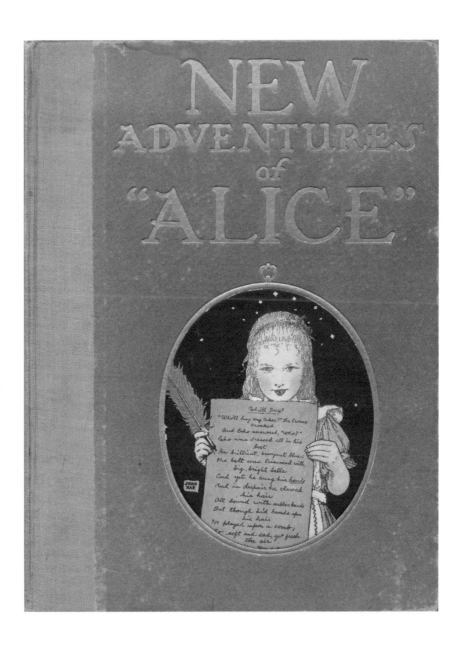

THE COVER OF THE 1917 EDITION

New Adventures of Alice

A sequel to
Lewis Carroll's Wonderland

by

John Rae

ILLUSTRATIONS BY
THE AUTHOR

evertype

2010

Published by Evertype, Cnoc Sceichín, Leac an Anfa, Cathair na Mart, Co. Mhaigh Eo, Éire. *www.evertype.com*.

This edition © 2010 Michael Everson.

First edition Chicago: P. F. Volland, 1917.

A catalogue record for this book is available from the British Library.

ISBN-10 1-904808-53-0
ISBN-13 978-1-904808-53-4

Typeset in De Vinne Text, Mona Lisa, ENGRAVERS' ROMAN, and *Liberty* by Michael Everson.

Cover: Michael Everson.

Printed by LightningSource.

Foreword

*J*ohn Rae (1882–1963) was born in Jersey City, New Jersey, and was educated at Pratt Institute High School in Brooklyn. In 1900 he attended the Art Students League of New York where he studied under illustrator and artist Howard Pyle. Of the better-known children's books Rae wrote and illustrated are *New Adventures of Alice, Grasshopper Green and The Meadow Mice,* and *Granny Goose.* More than fifty books, and many magazines of the day, sported Rae's illustrations. From 1935 to 1940, he taught Painting and Design at Rollins College in Winter Park, Florida. From the 1930s to the 1950s, Rae engaged in portraiture work, and notably painted the portraits of Carl Sandburg and Albert Einstein. Rae was a member of the Artists Guild, the Artists League of America, and the Society of American Illustrators, and was listed in *Who's Who in America* from 1926 to 1958.

Rae's book fulfils his own wish that Carroll had written another book about Wonderland. In it Alice visits a number of Mother Goose characters, as well as a remarkable artist, a poet, and a printer—characters certainly familiar to John Rae himself.

I have made a few editorial changes to John Rae's text of 1917, in order to bring it closer to modern tastes in format and language. I have normalized Rae's re-spelt "Gloster" and "Norrich" to "Gloucester" and "Norwich" since it seems to me that the re-spellings lack motivation. Carroll's example in similar cases. I have preferred the more modern "Yum, yum!" to "Um, um!", "Timbuktu" to "Timbucktoo", and "tureen" to "toureen". The term "snapper motto" on page 101 refers to the text on a slip of paper found in what is in Britain and Ireland known as a "(Christmas) cracker". Evidently these were somewhat more common in North America in 1917 than they are in 2010; the "fortunes" in Chinese fortune-cookies are perhaps the closest universally-known analogues today.

Where Rae follows Websterian spelling, I have altered to Oxford orthography: Alice is an English girl, after all. For the same reason, I favoured "holiday" to "vacation". In an attempt to bridge the Atlantic gap between "Lady Bugs" and "Ladybirds" I have settled for "Ladybird Beetles" which tends to be the modern scientific compromise. In places, Rae's punctuation has been altered to conform to modern practice. As in my other editions of Alice books, I have kept to the book design inspired by Martin Gardiner's *Annotated Alice*.

And, as usual, I have followed Carroll's preference in writing "ca'n't", "sha'n't", and "wo'n't".

Michael Everson
Westport, June 2010

Carroll, Lewis. 2000. *The Annotated Alice: Alice's Adventures in Wonderland & Through the Looking-Glass*. By Lewis Carroll; with original illustrations by John Tenniel. Updated, with an introduction and notes by Martin Gardiner. Definitive edition. New York & London: W. W. Norton & Company. ISBN 0-393-04847-0

Sigler, Carolyn. 1997. *Alternative Alices: Visions and revisions of Lewis Carroll's Alice books*. Lexington: University Press of Kentucky. ISBN 0-8131-2028-4

Sigler, Carolyn. 2008. "Alice Imitations" in *The Oxford Encyclopedia of Children's Literature*, vol. 1, pp 47–49. Oxford: Oxford University Press. ISBN 978-0-19-514656-1

New Adventures of Alice

CONTENTS

PREFACE TO THE 1917 EDITION

Probably you, like myself, have often wished that Lewis Carroll might have found time to write another book about *Alice*. Certainly most of the children who have delightedly followed her through *Wonderland* and the *Looking-Glass* country have sighed regretfully when Mother finished reading the last chapter to them.

After reading the marvelous tale for perhaps the tenth time when I was a little boy, I started trying to imagine what Lewis Carroll would have written had he continued the *Adventures*, and it has been great fun for me to go on with these imaginings from time to time and finally to write them down.

The children "with dreaming eyes of wonder" to whom I have related some of these *New Adventures* have frankly enjoyed them and their accompanying nonsense verses, and have helped with many stimulating questions and suggestions. This leads me to hope that even Lewis Carroll, himself, might have enjoyed some of these added "doings" of his adventurous *Alice*.

And so I make no excuse or apology for what to some may at first seem my shocking assurance, and if any of my love for the dear old dog-eared volume of *Alice's Adventures in Wonderland* and *Through the Looking-Glass* has crept—as I meant it should—between the lines of this humble supplement, that is excuse enough for its being. It is offered as a loving gift from thankful children to the sweet spirit of the immortal Lewis Carroll who has always seemed to me a dear, indulgent, story-telling Uncle to all children.

John Rae

John Rae
Caldwell, New Jersey

Dedication
For the many "Sisters and Brothers"—and
Grown-ups, too—who have loved
Alice and wished there
were more.

CHAPTER I

Found in the Attic

"But the provoking Kitten only began on the other paw, and pretended it hadn't heard the question. Which do *you* think it was?"

Mother closed the book and sister Betsy and brother Billy both sighed.

"Oh dear, I wish there were more of it," said Betsy. "Isn't there another book about Alice, Mother?"

It was the fifth or sixth time that Mother had read *Alice's Adventures in Wonderland* and *Through the Looking-Glass* to them out of the fat red book, and every time they had reached the end, Betsy had asked this same question.

"I'm just as sorry as you are, Dears, that there isn't," said Mother. "But even if there were we couldn't read any more tonight. It's your bed time!"

And sure enough, the old fashioned hall clock had begun to buzz and grind and click as it always did before striking

9

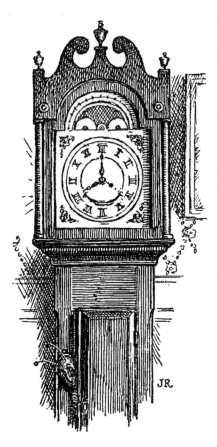

the hour. "As though it were chuckling wickedly to itself," Betsy thought.

Betsy must have been thinking of *Alice* and making up for herself more Adventures and wishing there were another book all the time she was getting undressed and brushing her nice little white teeth, for when she said her prayers she added, "And please send me another book about Alice."

She had hardly got comfortably snuggled and settled into the pillow and kissed Mother and called "Good night" to Dick, the canary (who answered with a sleepy little thrill), when she found herself up in the attic looking for things "to dress up in".

The bed-clothes seemed to have turned into dusty old dresses and coats which she was pulling over, looking for a little dress her Mother had worn when Mother herself was only eight years old. She knew it was somewhere in the pile of things in the attic, and would be just what she wanted to dress the part of *Alice*, in a little play which she and her brother and some of the other children were going to give, perhaps, the next Saturday afternoon.

Somehow or other the dresses and coats as she handled them became smaller and stiffer and smaller still and flat, and pretty soon she realized that they weren't dresses and coats at

all, but a pile of neat little books, none of which Betsy had ever seen before and which seemed to come in a sort of set. They were called "Wish There Were More" books or the "Sequel Series"—"Oh, if I only had them all on my shelves.

"Now," said Betsy to herself, "P'raps I'll find another Alice book." And she took them up one by one with eager hands.

There was *More Robinson Crusoe!*, *More Arabian Nights!*, *More Grimm's Fairy Tales!*, *More Wonder Clock Stories!*, and oh, dreams come true! there was the book she had longed for:—*More Adventures of Alice!*

She turned the pages with trembling fingers, afraid that she might find that it was a cruel joke: but no! There were exactly the same kind of stiff little pictures of Alice that she had loved in the battered old red book, from which Mother had just been reading. Alice doing this, or Alice doing that, and usually surrounded by strangely-dressed people or creatures.

With a sigh of complete contentment, she settled herself comfortably and cosily on a moth-eaten old buffalo robe in a corner nearest the half-moon attic window and started to read. In her dream she seemed to change and become dear, quaint little Alice herself, and be *living* and *acting* in the story, instead of simply reading it.

What follows is what she read, and the pictures that follow are those she looked at in that "Wish There Were More" book. For Betsy has often and often told me all about that wonderful dream of hers.

CHAPTER II

(Really Chapter I of the book Betsy found in the attic, in her dream)

To Bunberry Cross, or Along Came a Snipe

*I*t was a sleepy, spring-time Sunday afternoon. Alice was lying on the grass near the garden-house reading *Mother Goose Rhymes* to her kittens who were tumbling about near her in the slanting yellow sunshine. (She often pretended the kittens were small children.) Just now she was reading "Ding Dong Bell, Pussy's in the Well."

"I'm sure you'll like this one and it *may* prove a warning to you," she said.

Her sister was sitting on the garden-house step making a pretty little sketch of a blossoming hawthorne tree which stood in the corner of the hedge at the foot of the garden.

Over the hedge they could see the church spire across the river. Somewhere far off a bell was ringing. Its sweetly sleepy sound mingled with the scent of blossoms and the droning of Alice's voice very harmoniously.

She had just come to the line "What a naughty boy was that"—when she noticed a bird with a straw in its beak alighting on the hedge nearby. Alice stopped reading to watch him for she always liked to find out where nests were being built. The bird was a very sprightly little fellow, cocking his head from side to side and looking directly at Alice with remarkably intelligent bright eyes.

"Why," thought Alice, "he looks as if he were actually going to speak!"

And sure enough, he did!

"Wonderful view from here," said the bird casually in a rather muffled voice. Alice now saw it was a Snipe, much larger than she had at first supposed, and that instead of a straw he held in his beak a long clay pipe from which a thin

wisp of bluish smoke was curling, and which probably caused the indistinct mumbling voice.

The hedge, too, seemed to be changing strangely, it was growing higher and higher, and soon she saw it was a hedge no longer, but a grove of tall oaks, and the muffled voice of the Snipe now sounded very far away indeed.

"I've something important to ask you. Do you—" she thought she heard him say and then she could not catch any more, though he was still to be seen on one of the topmost branches of the tree nearest her.

Now Alice was a very polite little girl, and it seemed to her that the only right thing for her to do was to climb the tree and find out what it was that the Snipe wished to know. So she was very pleased to see a narrow spiral stairway, which she had certainly not noticed before, winding up around the trunk. She placed her foot upon the lowest step and grasped the rail,

and was greatly surprised to find that the railing seemed to be moving spirally upward; pulling her along, at first slowly and gently but getting faster and faster, so that by the time she was half way up the tree her feet were no longer touching the steps at all. Somehow though, the sensation was rather pleasant and she felt no alarm. She even kept calm enough to notice that, as the trunk apparently slid down past her, little bird faces appeared at open, curtained windows here and there, and one old-lady black-bird in a blue sunbonnet called out as Alice shot past—"Hoity, toity, my dear child, there's *really* no such hurry, you know."

Faster and faster she went, so that when the tree-top was reached she could not seem to stop, but went right on up into the air quite a ways and then gently floated down (her skirt spreading out like a parachute and supporting her) and finally alighted on the topmost branch, right beside the Snipe.

Talking to the Snipe was a curious little fellow with a big, round, shiny face and very slender little legs and arms. In one hand he carried a covered basket and in the other a big blue handkerchief, decorated with little white stars. In his belt was a great cheese knife. His round face was shining with perspiration and from time to time he mopped it with the blue handkerchief.

"He looks as though he had come a long way," thought Alice.

As she settled herself on the swaying branch and smoothed out her skirt, the Snipe was saying thoughtfully, puffing hard on his pipe, "Norwich, Norwich?—Now—let—me—see—I *should* know, and that's a fact—Perhaps *she* can tell you!" he exclaimed, brightening.

The Man in the Moon (for of course Alice knew now that it must be he) turned respectfully to her. "Your pardon, Miss, but could you, perhaps, tell me as how I could get to Norwich? I'm anxious to get there before nightfall, that I am, Miss."

"He speaks exactly like the nice old farmer who comes around to sell us cheese," thought Alice.

"And that's just what he does," put in the Snipe, just as if she had said it aloud. "Of course, you know," he continued, "the moon's made of green cheese and," pointing to the Man in the Moon, "he peddles it. Give her a sample."

Little bird faces appeared at open, curtained windows.

"'Certingly, Miss, to be sure," beamed the Man in the Moon, "and no obligation to buy neither, Miss."

He opened his basket and taking his knife from his belt cut off a thin slice of the most beautiful and curious cheese that Alice had ever seen. It was soft and glowed with a greenish-silver light, and when she bit into it! "It was like eating marshmallows dipped in moonlight," she said afterwards.

Alice was just about to take a second bite when she remembered that the Moon Man's courteous question had not been answered, and she started to direct him as well as she could; but somehow her geography lessons and some directions she had heard the gardener give a wagon driver the day before became hopelessly mixed in her mind and she found herself saying, "Norwich is a town of seven thousand inhabitants in the north eastern part of Norfolk on the river Yare. You take the road to the right as far as Earle's Bridge and follow the river to the old Exton Mill—settled in the year thirteen hundred and forty—turn to the left and the principal exports are—" She stopped, realizing how absurdly she was talking and intending to say, "No, that's not at all what I meant."

But the jolly little man had already started. He was not flying, but stepping briskly along "on nothing at all", swinging his basket, and Alice could just hear him anxiously repeating part of her ridiculous directions—"to old Exton Mill, settled in thirteen hundred and forty—"

She called after him, but he evidently did not hear for he kept straight ahead and soon disappeared behind a great flock of black-birds.

The Snipe shook his head sadly and blew tremendous puffs of whirling smoke from his pipe in silence for a while, but finally he sighed—"Poor fellow! *Poor* fellow, but I dare say he'll happen on the finger-post and then he can get to *Babylon* anyhow; that is, of course, if he has a candle about him."

"What good would *that* do him?" asked Alice, anxiously, for she was quite worried about the Man in the Moon. She naturally felt responsible and guilty. Of course, she hadn't really meant to give him those absurd directions. "I don't believe I even got the population right," she said to herself, helplessly.

"Why, silly, you can always get to Babylon by candle light," replied the Snipe, severely. "And you ought to know it. Great view," he added absently, as if to change the subject.

Now for the first time Alice looked down. How changed everything was! The gravel garden path had become a dusty road winding under the oaks, and in place of her sister there was a strange little man in very baggy clothes and a flowing necktie so long that the ends hung down almost to the ground. He was busily sketching just as her sister had been.

Alice, although she was ever so high up in the tree-tops, could somehow or other see just what he was drawing on his little pad. This was what she saw:—

"Why, it's the Old Lady 'with Rings on her Fingers and Bells on Her Toes', just like the picture in my *Mother Goose*," she exclaimed delightedly.

"Yes, he drew us all, drat him," murmured the Snipe, crossly. "He made one of my wings shorter than the other, too!"

When the artist's picture was finished it seemed immediately to grow to natural size and come to life.

By this time Alice was quite used to unusual happenings, and about the only thing that could have startled her very much would have been for something to look "just everydayish" or act in a perfectly normal manner. She was not at all surprised, therefore, to see the white hobby horse start off down the road with a rocking sort of gait, the old lady in her familiar spotted dress and strange bonnet jouncing up and down on his back and in a cloud of dust.

Alice could just catch the faint jingling of the "bells on her toes".

"This must be the road to Banbury Cross, then," said Alice, half aloud.

"*Bun*berry Cross," corrected the Snipe, kindly. "No fault of yours, my child, the Printer ran out of U's, that's all. You see it's where they make the hot cross berry-buns. You'd never say, 'hot cross *bans*'. No, certainly not! In the first place it would never rhyme with *sons*, and in the second pla—but no matter. What do you think of the view?"

And pointing to the artist with his pipe, "He drew it all—all the houses and trees and the hills just as he had to draw all of us, birds and animals and people."

Now Alice knew why it was that the landscape looked "strangely familiar"; it, too, was like the pictures in her *Mother*

Goose! But also quite a little like Wonderland and the strange Looking-Glass country that she had once dreamt about.

"Isn't it hilly?" Alice began. "And what's that—"

"Of course! It has to be hilly," interrupted the Snipe, impatiently. "There's got to be Jack and Jill's Hill and

Blackbird's Hill and the Hill the Old Woman lived under and Pippin Hill and all the rest of the Hills."

Now, ever since Alice had reached the tree-top, a far-away bell had been ringing, just as one had rung before she left the garden and her sister and the Kittens. (And dear, dear! How long ago that did seem.) Alice wondered idly what the bell could be.

"It's the bellman over at Bunberry Cross, I'm pretty sure," said the Snipe, who always seemed good at guessing just what one was going to say. "Probably somebody's stolen something or other and the King has offered a reward for the capture of the thief. There're lots of thieves among 'em, Tom, the Piper's Son, who stole the pig, and dozens more. Why, even one of their Kings, years ago, stole some barley meal for a bag pudding!"

"What a bad example!" exclaimed Alice.

"Let's go and see what the row's about," suggested the Snipe. "I've got to return this pipe anyway. Of course that pipe business was just a practical joke. I hope you didn't think *I* was a thief." He looked anxiously at Alice, then added more brightly, "Bombay's the next village beyond and the Old Man's a great friend of King Cole's—in fact, he's Prime Minister.

"Let's start—Ever fly?"

Before Alice realized what was happening, the Snipe had given her a gentle push and she found herself awkwardly floundering about in the air, not exactly frightened but a bit cross that the Snipe should have given her no warning.

"Well, I don't think *that* was very nice and I did so want to see what the artist was going to draw next," said she.

"It's the only way to ever learn to fly or swim," said the Snipe, amiably but decidedly. "Try it more this way—that's better." And then as if to put her in a better humour he began to sing—as well as possible with the pipe still in his mouth:—

"You never know what you can do till you try;
A girl like a bird may be able to fly;
A bird like a fly may be able to buzz;
Things stranger have happened and every day does.
I've heard many times (I have proofs if you wish)
A deaf and dumb oyster can sing like a fish!—"

"But fish ca'n't sing," interrupted Alice, who by this time was managing to fly fairly well and was going remarkably fast—she had to keep a little ahead of the Snipe, as the smoke trailing from the pipe was very choking and blinding.

"What's their scales for then, I'd like to know?" snapped the Snipe; and after a moment he added, triumphantly, "Some of 'em fly anyhow! But don't interrupt again or we'll never get there."

Alice couldn't see just what the song had to do with getting them there, but said nothing, and the bird continued—

"Why how, let me ask you, my dear, do you s'pose
I learned to smoke pipes, and to eat with my nose?
There's one thing, however, that cannot be done
With all of your trying, that's this—
Have a bun."

The strangest thing had happened! They were "bumping into a flock of buns" as the Snipe expressed it. The air was full of hot cross buns which seemed to be floating up from an open window of a house on the outskirts of the village far below them.

"That's the baker's shop and there's the butcher's and there's the candlestick maker's," said the Snipe.

Alice saw that they were now right over a little village. She had been too busy listening to the Snipe to realize how fast they had approached it.

"Drop 'em a penny, drop 'em a penny!" called the Snipe, and then in his effort to snatch one of the floating buns with his beak lost the pipe which fell through the air, leaving behind it a trail of blue smoke.

"Now I'm in a pretty pickle and no mistake," he mumbled in a scared voice. "I didn't mean to keep the old pipe, it was just a joke—"

"But here we are!" cried Alice between bites—she had caught two of the buns which were still very warm and wonderfully light. "Perhaps that's why they float away," she thought.

"Yes, here we are!"

And, sure enough, they were hovering directly over the village green where a May-pole stood decked out with streamers and flowers ready for the dance. It was just like one Alice had seen a few days before on their village green at home.

Then she saw that the bell, whose ding donging had been growing louder and louder as they had approached the village, was being rung by the Bellman or "Town Crier" who stopped his ringing now and then to bawl out:

> *"Has anyone seen Master Thomas B. Green?*
> *Be he dead or alive, the reward is two 'n five!"*

"Let's stop here," said Alice, clutching at the May-pole to stop her flight. (You see she had never practised alighting gracefully.)

She swung round and round and round and round. Petals from the blossom wreaths were shaken off and floated down all about her. When she softly struck the ground after her long spiral descent no one seemed to have noticed her, for the Bellman was the centre of attraction. All the strange townsfolk and animals were crowding about him listening to his bawling, or talking together in excited groups.

When she looked about her for the Snipe he was nowhere to be seen, but finally she spied him perched on the very top of the May-pole. He seemed agitated and was whispering something hoarsely to her, but she could only make out the words—"Don't dare to come down" and "They'll put me in jail" and "I'll see you some time again"—Then he flapped heavily away and Alice suddenly felt very lonesome and just a little scared.

CHAPTER III

The Peevish Printer

"It makes me sick! Absolutely sick!" exclaimed a small peevish voice at Alice's elbow. "They ought to have let me print 'em some neat handbills to stick up at every corner instead of having all this hubbub."

Turning, Alice saw a little spectacled man almost bald, with a very inky apron and the dirtiest hands she had ever seen. She simply couldn't help looking at them a little disapprovingly, as her Mother looked at *hers* sometimes.

He did not seem to notice her reproving glance, however, but continued to exclaim, "It makes me sick!" more bitterly than before, now putting his hands over his ears as if to shut out the din made by the Town Crier's bawling and the noisy bell. Of course when he did this his ears and cheeks became almost as dirty as his hands, and Alice found herself saying, "Now just look at your face!"

"Don't be ridiculous," said the little man. "How can I look at my face? That's for *you* to do! There are no mirrors in this town anyhow, even if I *wanted* to look at my face, which I don't. You see King Cole—but that's a long story, perhaps I have it with me.

"I'm a Printer, as you may have guessed; that is, I'm a Printer *most* of the time. *Fair time* I sell pies—have to make a living *somehow*, you know."

"Oh, then you're the Pieman!" exclaimed Alice.

"Yes—but Pastry Purveyor would have sounded much better, don't you think so? Looked well in print, too."

He had been fumbling in his pocket and now fished out a folded sheet of very soiled paper which he carefully spread out on the grass.

"This isn't it, I'm afraid," he murmured, "but it will do *pretty* well."

It was the strangest page of print Alice had ever seen. She could make nothing of it except the title at the top which was PRINTER'S PI—in very black capital letters.

"But even that's spelled wrong," she said to herself. "It should be PI*E*."

The rest was a jumble of letters and figures and punctuation marks of all kinds and sizes, something like this:—

☞
```
              PRINTER'S PI
:7xumllq   „ffneosn6uri   fussiop
8—..  4pa55  n%@W  (h;TP  #9
:beic?SI.  −S  pvhr−5.  X  ufram
tuPl#7.−)−vdgsyainby        PT.;$£
tcb yjO : ;  bf hyS  RVTG  Y#3−4(7
.a,Ohf6%cRVhin#2.yuth43´/:p
.19n?b6h5g4c$2x −invbg
```

"Perhaps it's a puzzle?"

"It looks very interesting and like some foreign language," said Alice, doubtfully. "But what *does* it mean?"

"That's what I was hoping *you'd* be able to tell *me*," said the Printer, thoughtfully tapping the paper as though to shake the jumble of letters into some more readable arrangement.

"Children usually know all about pie. You see, I have to print this sort of thing now and then just to keep busy now that they have a Town Crier," he added apologetically.

"I wish I had a piece of *apple* pie right this minute," sighed Alice, suddenly reminded that she was very hungry in spite of the two flying buns she had eaten.

"You *ought* to've come at Fair time you know," said the Printer. "But perhaps we can manage it, it's only a matter of spelling after all."

He drew from the huge pocket in his apron a very compactly folded-up little printing press and some small sheets of paper; found an E—which he inked with the palm of his hand—and printed it carefully after the PI of the title, making it PIE.

'They're kicking up such a noise I almost forgot how to spell," he muttered to himself. "Don't want to see you go hungry, though, and I'll do the best I can for you. But show me first your penny," he added absent-mindedly.

While he talked he had been tearing the paper into the form of scalloped circle like this:—

—and finally handed it to her.

Alice was somehow not in the least surprised that the paper pie had become brown and warm and fragrant and the letters P I E had turned into the usual row of cuts in the crust.

She handed him a penny which he took and examined with great interest turning it over and over and murmuring in a hoarse whisper—"Very pretty—very pretty—a good likeness, too—very good indeed."

Alice had noticed that his voice had been growing hoarser and hoarser as he talked. It was now scarcely audible.

When he had thoroughly examined the coin he put it back into her hand, pushing it away without a word when she tried to return it to him. He then started setting type with great rapidity and slipping a small piece of paper into the press he jammed down the lever, raised it again and pulled out this neatly printed little slip:

> I said, "*show* me your penny"
> Not, "*give* me your penny."

"Oh!" said Alice. "So you did."

This seemed to her a strange way of carrying on a conversation but, "After all," she said to herself, "it's really a very nice sort of a game. I wonder if he usually talks this way?"

The Printer seemed to have read her thoughts, for in the twinkling of an eye he had printed another little slip like this:—

> Well, in the first place, as you see, my voice is rather weak;
> It very rapidly becomes a whisper, so to speak.
> Just think how handy it might be to print, instead of talk,
> If I should fall into the sea:
>   "Help! Help!" I'd never squawk.
> Not I, I'd print some circulars
>   (In bold faced type display)
>   **"Your kind assistance is required;
>   I'm sinking in the bay."**
> Or, if I took to me a wife,
>   Stone deaf; of course, you see
> In converse, then, how indispensable my press would be!

"That sounds very reasonable, I must say," mused Alice.

> Of *course* it's reasonable

said (or rather printed) the peevish Printer, petulantly; then
something seemed to occur to him. He smiled mysteriously
and printed this—("That tiny type looks just like a whisper,"
thought Alice).

> This is a secret!
> I'm the man who printed Mother Goose! This is a rhyme the Poet wrote about me.
>   Printer Man, Printer Man, print me a book;
>   Tell what a great Man am I;
>   Make me a Hero, by hook or by crook,
>   Or I'll beat you and blacken your eye!
> I didn't just like that one (especially the part about beating me) so I simply left it
> out. You see I might have been twice as famous. There's just that Pie-Man rhyme
> about me now. Then, too, I wasn't anxious to be known as the Printer of the book
> either. The poet who wrote the rhymes has had to live in hiding for years. (Some folks
> didn't like what he said about 'em and wanted to kill him) and they might have felt
> the same about me for printing what he wrote. I don't know as I'm exactly proud of
> being classed with that Mother Goose crowd anyway, they're a mixed lot; beggars,
> pigs, and pipers and very few gentlemen among 'em, you'll notice.

Alice *had* noticed that the crowd gathered about the Town
Crier in the street was a strangely assorted lot (though all
looked familiar), tall and short, fat and thin, beggars and fine

folk, and a great many quaintly-dressed old women and children. Pigs, cats, dogs and crows and other beasts and birds seemed to mingle with the rest on equal terms. One neatly-shaven pig she noticed coming out of a shop, over the door of which hung a sign:—

She had been so interested in the printed conversation game that she had almost forgotten to eat her pie which lay on the grass beside them. Now she took it up.

"What a dear little brown pie! How good it will taste!" she thought. "Yum, yum! I'd better eat it before it's all cold," she thought, and politely started to offer a bite to the Printer, but saw that he was furiously busy printing a lot of little circulars on bright red paper!

When he had printed fifty or more he gathered them up and jumped to his feet. Then thrusting one into Alice's hand so excitedly that he caused her to drop the pie, he dashed off into the crowd distributing his red circulars right and left in mad haste. Even the Bellman stopped his din in amazement.

Alice looked at the scarlet sheet and read in huge capitals—

FIRE!!   FIRE!!!
FIRE!!!!

CHAPTER IV

Fire!!

$\mathcal{A}$ll was confusion and excitement! Some of the Mother Goose people were running in one direction and some in another. Most of the crowd were trying to squeeze through the town-gate and seemed to be hopelessly stuck in the narrow opening.

While Alice stood wondering in which direction the fire really lay, she noticed nearby a little man in green pointing excitedly with a long flute. Looking in the direction in which he was pointing she saw, through an opening between the bakery and the barber shop a thin column of smoke which seemed to come from behind a barn in a field about half a mile away.

"That must be it," thought Alice, "for where there's smoke there must be fi—."

Just then somebody collided with her so violently that she was almost knocked off her feet!

"I beg your pardon, Miss, but really you know, Miss, you should be more careful 'ow you stands about staring—that was, as you might say, a close shave. I might 'ave cut yer hear off."

It was the Barber. He held a large nicked razor and a mug of lather in one hand and an unfinished wig in the other. He was very much confused and flustered by the collision and began to mutter, "I'll never get it done. I'll never get it done, that I wo'n't. Something halways hinterrupts."

He seemed *so* unhappy that Alice, wishing to divert his mind, bethought herself of the pie and politely offered him a bite. "Thankee, Miss," said the Barber, brightening. "A pinch or two—a pinch or two—it's just wot I needs."

Puzzled by his words, Alice looked down at the pie and saw to her surprise that it was a pie no longer but a very large round snuff box, the cover of which still slightly resembled a piecrust, being made of yellow ivory, inlaid with flying blackbirds; the edge was scalloped.

"You're werry kind, Miss, I'm sure, you're werry kind indeed. Though I'm bound to say," he added, "as how *ladies* doesn't *usually* carry—"

"Look!" cried Alice. "Who are *they*?"

Two quaint figures, a boy and a girl, were coming down the street in long leaps. It seemed to be a sort of race and the strange girl, who had just cleared the May-pole in a tremendous jump, was slightly in the lead. "It'll be Jumping-Joan and Jack-be-Nimble, of course, Miss, they always gets to fires first," muttered the Barber complainingly. And then, struck by a bright idea, he shouted at the fast approaching figures, "Give us a lift! Give us a lift!" And turning to Alice, "'Itch on and 'old tight!"

The next moment Alice found herself clinging to Jack-be-Nimble's hand and leaping with him over the candlestick maker's shop. "Just like big grasshoppers," she said to herself.

Soon they could see the fire distinctly.

"It's the King's haystack, just as I thought!" said Jack, excitedly, "and we ought to be the first ones there. I hope that big barn near the stack doesn't catch fire, for all the King's horses are in *there*."

"Maybe Boy Blue has been playing with matches," ventured Alice. "That looks like the pictures of the haystack he always takes his nap in."

"Listen! There's the new fire-alarm," cried Jack, bounding along in his excitement faster than ever, so that they really seemed not to touch the ground at all. "It's the Cat, you know. He's paid by the town according to the amount of noise he makes, and," he added with a happy sigh, "he *can* make a *delicious* amount when he really tries—he plays a fiddle and a pair of bagpipes at the same time!"

"Oh, there he comes now, out of the barn!" cried Alice as the caterwauling din rose louder and more piercing. "And *look* at the fire *now*! Do you think—"

"It was all our fault, too," interrupted a familiar voice at her elbow, in a hoarse stage-whisper. She turned to see the

It seemed to be a sort of race.

Snipe who was flying along by her side; he seemed very much agitated and there was an air of mystery about him. "That is to say," he continued, "it's *really* the Baker's fault you know, for if *he* hadn't let those buns escape and fly away, *we* never would have dropped that dratted pipe." Here the Snipe hesitated a moment, looked this way and that, then getting very close to Alice's ear whispered louder than before, "*It must have been that pipe that set fire to the King's haystack!* If the Prime Minister finds it out *we'll* go to the dungeons, of course."

"I don't quite see why he says, '*We* shouldn't have dropped the pipe', and '*We'll* go to the dungeons'," thought Alice. "*I* had nothing to do with it, I'm sure." She had begun to feel very impolite not to have introduced Jack-be-Nimble to the Snipe. Then too it seemed extremely rude for the Snipe to continue whispering to her and ignoring her companion.

"Have you met my friend—" she began; but when she turned it was quite a different person from her leaping partner of a few moments before whose hand she now held. He was a strange little spindle-legged man, rather shabby, with *very* long hair, large wistful eyes and a friendly smile.

"I'm the Poet. Jack was only a disguise. Have to do it, or they'd get me, I surmise," said he, pointing back at the crowd they had left far behind.

Alice, the Snipe, and the Poet were now walking hurriedly across a broad stubbly field toward the burning haystack. As they approached, a cloud of Ladybird Beetles passed over them, coming from the direction of the fire. "Poor things," said the Snipe, remorsefully to himself. "They probably lived in that haycock."

"Let's watch the blaze awhile from here, until the townsfolk get too near," suggested the Poet smiling at Alice and added, "Then we must skip, you know, my dear, all three of us have cause to fear!"

Alice now noticed for the first time that the little man wore a brass chain about his neck with a metal tag, numbered 333; she wondered what it could possibly be, but was, of course, far too polite to ask on such short acquaintance.

"My Poet's License—as you see, my number is three-thirty-three," the Poet remarked pleasantly, noticing her curiosity. "A thing I'm very proud of too—becoming, *quite*, I think. Don't you?"

All this time the smoke from the hay was growing blacker and thicker, and the din of the fire-alarm bag-pipes was getting louder and wilder and the scraping of the cat's fiddle more shrill and piercing.

Now from the big barn nearby came sounds of trampling feet and ungrammatical shouts of "That's him! That's him! There he is!" And what seemed to Alice like *hundreds* of archers, each with a big gold crown embroidered on his left sleeve, rushed pell-mell out of the big barn door.

"We're lost! Alack-a-day, friends, we must flee! All the King's men! I know they're after me," exclaimed the Poet.

"It's *me* they're after, neighbour, if you must know," said the Snipe a little jealously. "*I* dropped the pipe that caused this fire in the King's hay."

Alice was a little frightened, it must be confessed, and *very* impatient at the Poet and the Snipe for waiting to talk when it did seem as though they should all have been running for their lives!

The Archers had drawn up in line in front of the barn and one who seemed to be their captain stepped forward and gave the commands, "Ready!—Aim!—"

The Poet turned to Alice excitedly and whispered very rapidly, "I have a plan. We'll wait until they shoot; each grab a shaft and out of danger scoot, then—"

"Fire!" yelled the captain of the King's men, and the air was full of flying arrows.

"All aboard! Don't be slow. Hold on tight! Home we go," shouted the Poet.

Whirrrr—an arrow whizzed by close to Alice's head, and following the suggestion of the Poet, she grasped it as it flew past and scrambled aboard. "An *arrow* escape," she heard the Snipe chuckle. The goose-feather tip made a very comfortable springy seat and she could hold firmly to the shaft near the head.

The arrow was going at a frightful speed, and the Wind whistled behind Alice's ears; in fact, it whistled a real tune, "*London Bridge*". "And very prettily too," thought Alice. "I wonder if '*Blue Bells of Scotland*' comes next, as it does on my music box?"

She had just turned to see if the Poet and Snipe were anywhere near her when suddenly everything grew black as night and she realized that they had dived into the thick cloud of smoke from the fire.  Alice clutched the arrow tighter. "For," she said to herself, "it *would* be nasty to fall into the fire with this clean pinafore on."

Somehow the shaft of the arrow had grown

softer and feathery and when Alice looked down she saw that it was now a fat grey goose she rode! The goose seemed to have lost her way in the dense smoke and was flying hither and thither in an aimless fashion.

The smoky darkness was full of sparks. "Or are they stars?" she wondered. "And isn't that the light from a little window way off there?" The goose seemed to have seen the lighted window too, for she stopped darting about and flew very rapidly in that direction, murmuring half under her breath, "That's the house I'm sure, I smell the cakes a-burning."

As they came nearer Alice saw that the light came from a tiny little thatched cottage, built high in the air, on four tremendously long poles.

"Why it's all upstairs," she exclaimed.

"To prove that I'm erratic, I built my house all attic," said a voice near at hand; and there was the Poet flying along beside her on a goose exactly like hers.

S e l f - S t e e r i n g P e n s

*B*y the time they had reached the front door of the strange little four-legged house and alighted, the smoke had all cleared away. Instead of sparks, the sky was full of wonderfully brilliant stars, thickly spread and so carefully arranged in their constellations that one could easily pick out the Great Bear, the Little Bear and all the rest; the Dragon was *so* real that Alice was almost frightened for the moment. "It's just like the chart in Uncle's big Astronomy," she cried, clapping her hands.

The Poet turned to Alice and said earnestly, "If the Dipper were nearer 'twould do very well (perhaps you have noticed a scorched sort of smell!) but we're short here of water, so far from the ground, and cakes *always* burn if I just turn around."

He had been fumbling with a curious big brass key that hung at his belt and had finally managed, by trying it backwards, to push it into the keyhole and turn the lock which sprung to with a loud report.

"There, that's locked now, so let's go in. It's time our supper to begin," he murmured, and then dived in through an open window!

It seemed, to Alice, a strange performance to carefully lock the door and enter by the window, but she was getting used to surprises of all sorts.

"I suppose he *has* a reason," she decided and followed. In so doing she knocked over a huge bottle of ink which had been standing on a little desk near the window.

Alice was a very neat little girl and anything of this sort distressed her almost beyond words.

"Oh dear! *Now* I've done it," she wailed as the ink, which was bright green, ran down over the stool and onto the floor. She started desperately mopping it up with her hand-kerchief but this seemed useless, as by this time it was at least an inch deep all over the floor!

"No matter—an accident—worry no more, but just take a look at my ink-saving floor," remarked the Poet casually, turning from the stove where he had been mournfully examining the burned remnants of the patty-cakes through a large reading glass.

"It happens so often—about once a day—that week ago Wednesday I fixed it *this* way," he added, and raised a small trap-door in the middle of the floor. Alice now saw that the floor was full of shallow grooves which led the ink to a little well under the trapdoor. Soon the last drop had run into the inkwell.

The Poet now went over to what looked like a sort of an umbrella-stand which was full of enormous quill pens, and selecting a beautiful bright blue one, he handed it politely to Alice, taking a green one with yellow spots for himself. He then took from a drawer, in the little desk, some very long narrow sheets of bright crimson paper, remarking with a chuckle, as he held them up, "It's *easily read*, as somebody said."

Sitting crosslegged on the floor, the Poet dipped his pen into the inkwell and started to write rapidly.

"Try it! Try it! Don't sit quiet," he cried, pushing several sheets of the crimson paper toward Alice and excitedly running his fingers through his long hair. Alice noticed that even when he did this the big quill-pen kept on writing busily, making a wonderful flourish at the end of each verse and occasionally adding a "Spencerian swan" for good measure!

Alice dipped *her* pen in the bright green ink and was delighted to find that it started immediately to write in a neat rounded script, fairly dragging her small hand along with it.

"We may as well finish up Volume Eight! *No supper tonight*, says the voice of Fate," muttered the Poet after he had written

a verse or two, adding, after a moment's reflection, "Though I'm not sure I shall ever dare to publish these. I must have a care."

Alice hardly heard a word of what the Poet was saying, for she was fascinated by the very unusual sensation of using a "self-steering pen", and *tremendously* interested to see what it would write.

"Of course it will be all nonsense," she said to herself, and nonsense it surely was. After a minute or two the blue quill stopped and this was what she read:

ECHO

> *"Who'll buy my cakes?" the crocus*
> *croaked.*
> *And Echo answered, "Who?"*
> *Echo was dressed all in his best*
> *In brilliant, buoyant blue.*
> *His belt was trimmed with big bright*
> *bells,*
> *And yet he wrung his hands,*
> *And in despair he clawed his hair,*
> *All bound with rubber bands,*
> *Yet though he'd bands upon his hair*
> *He played upon a comb!*
> *The air was fresh and soft and sad,*
> *Somewhat like "Homb, Sweet*
> *Homb,"*
> *Though this fresh air was all about,*
> *He breathed a last farewell.*
> *"Who'll buy my cakes?" the crocus*
> *croaked;*
> *For he had soap to sell."*

The Poet scratched his head judicially for a moment then said slowly, "That's *rather* good, yes rather *good*, but really now I think I should leave out that part about the cake, it almost makes one's stomach ache. Though, if one makes of it a lather, soap's not bad eating—if you'd *rather*. Let's see if *this* one's worth its ink—the *title's* pleasing—'Come to Think'."

The Poet then started to read from the sheet he was holding—

> *"COME TO THINK"*
> *Why is it ZEBRA's sometimes spelled with double X and*
> *Y?*
> *I don't know, but I'll ask Aunt Ann, perhaps SHE'LL tell*
> *me why.*
> *And why, you ask me, does a dog face always nor'-nor'*
> *west?*
> *I cannot answer THAT although I've tried my level best.*
> *And why, oh why, do you and I*
> *Walk on our thumbs and ears?*
> *I do not know, YOU do not know,*
> *THEY do not know, my dears.*
> *WHY is a porpoise always PINK?*
> *I'll try hard to recall—*
> *Why—come to think, THEY'RE NEVER PINK,*
> *THEY'RE NEVER PINK AT ALL!*

"That'll *do*, I guess," said the Poet doubtfully, setting the sheet aside. "It's got a good moral, anyway." Alice couldn't exactly see just where the moral came but she didn't interrupt to ask about it, for the Poet had already begun to chuckle over another sheet which he soon started to read as follows:—

They seek the Wurbaloo.

SECRETS

Come close to me, that I to you a secret may impart;
A secret more important, too, than how to toss a tart.
I'll whisper in your purple ear, like this, a word or two.
Come nearer, lest THEY *overhear;*
THEY seek the Wurbaloo!
At three o'clock I heard them creep, at four I heard them
  crawl,
At five-fifteen in silence deep I—"
DONG! DONG!! DONG!!!

Alice jumped to her feet in alarm, for a sudden deafening sound of bells filled the tiny room.

"Whoa there! BACK! Dobbin—Jack," shouted the Poet over his shoulder in a matter-of-fact way. Alice looking in the direction of the furious ringing saw that it came from bells on the collars of two tiny dappled horses who had stepped out onto a little platform under the face of a very curiously-carved clock like a toy stable, which hung in the corner of the room.

"Well," said Alice, much relieved, "that *is* a strange sort of cuc-koo-clock."

"It's not *cuc-koo-clock*, my dear. Those are *bell horses* that you hear."

"One o'clock, two o'clock, off and away," quoted Alice.

"Yes," shouted the Poet, for the bells were still jangling loudly.

"At two o'clock the Beggars always come, and we have nothing for 'em, not a crumb. And hark! I think I hear another bell, that must be Pussy, once more down the well. You jump on Dobbin and I'll take old Jack and off we'll go before—"

At this moment the Snipe, whom Alice had almost forgotten, poked his head in the little window and whispered hoarsely, "Quick! They're coming! Don't you hear the dogs barking? Run for it!"

CHAPTER VI

It's a Dangerous Place

Almost before the Snipe had finished his warning, Alice found herself mounted on one of the dappled bell-horses and galloping along at a furious pace on a dark road which wound in and out through a very dismal forest of twisted, bare trees.

The bell on her horse's collar made a terrifying amount of noise in the silent woods.

"I'm sure the Beggars will hear it and know where I am," said Alice half aloud. She finally managed to reach down over the horse's neck and tie her handkerchief about the bell-clapper. She could now hear the watch-dogs barking far in the rear and had just settled herself quite comfortably in the big wooden saddle when a friendly voice behind her panted, "I say—wait up a bit—ca'n't you? *What's* your hurry? Though for that matter I'm usually in a hurry myself. It keeps you busy this being a hero, always running about—to drowning accidents and affairs of that sort."

The owner of the voice had now caught up with Alice who was pulling in the bell-horse as well as she could. Looking down she saw a short, very fat little fellow, dripping wet from head to foot, running along beside her as fast as his ridiculously short chubby legs would carry him. Under his arm he carried a small white kitten ("Just like my own Pussikins," thought Alice—) which was wetter, if possible, than he.

"There's nothing for you to be afraid of now that *I'm* here," he continued cheerily. "I'm sure the Beggars would never dare to follow you into *this* forest anyhow, for they know it's a dangerous place and full of dangerous people. The Raven lives here," he continued in his gossipy way, "the one with the frightful voice, you know, and the Old-Man-who-wouldn't-say-his-Prayers and John O'Gudgeon, the Wild-Man, and Peg's father, the Miller, and Margery Daw—and the Four and Twenty Tailors—though of course *they're* not so *very* dangerous," he added reassuringly, for Alice was beginning to look just a bit frightened.

"Don't you think you'd better get up behind me and ride a ways?" she suggested, for the roly-poly little fellow was beginning to puff from his exertions in keeping up with the galloping bell-horse; and anyhow, it would be rather a comfort, she thought, under the circumstances to have such a hero as Johnny Stout near her for a while, at least.

He assented very readily, and handing Alice the bedraggled White Kitten, clambered up panting.

The further they rode into the wood the darker it became. The trees were now so tall and the branches so interwoven that no sky was to be seen. From these gnarled black branches hung long grey moss like the threadbare garments of ugly old giants. "In fact, I'm not at all sure that they *are* really trees and *not* ogres of some sort," said Alice to herself.

Once or twice she looked back over her shoulder and it was very disturbing to notice that the trees had apparently closed in behind them and seemed to be standing in the road pointing at her and whispering together. In these rather terrifying surroundings it was a comfort to have the little White Kitten to hug, damp though it was.

"Its purring sounds very homelike," thought Alice.

"Must be long past tea time, and this riding gives a chap an *awful* appetite," sighed Johnny Stout, after they had gone what seemed miles and miles. It was now almost pitch dark. "We'll soon be at the mill though, and if you'll just pretend you've a wooden leg we *may* get a dumpling or two."

Alice was about to ask for an explanation of this puzzling remark when she caught sight of a lighted window through the trees ahead and heard the clattering and creaking of a mill-wheel.

"What a strange place for a mill here in this deep forest!" she exclaimed. "But perhaps it's a *saw*-mill."

"You're *almost* right," said Johnny, "but not exactly. It's an axe-mill. A place where they grind axes, you know; they have to have axes to cut down trees to make axe helves, to say nothing of the jack-straws and tooth-picks they make from the smaller pieces."

As they drew nearer they heard loud harsh voices raised in angry dispute.

"They're always at it," said Johnny. "Never saw such a family for fighting. You see the Old Miller has dyspepsia, and no wonder, he lives on crab-apple dumplings!"

By this time they had almost reached the mill, the door of which now burst violently open. Out hopped a dishevelled young woman with a wooden leg, followed closely by an ugly bald old man who stopped just outside the door to hurl a huge, heavy-looking dumpling at her. "What did I tell you?" chuckled Johnny, "That old—"

CAW! CA-AW!! CA-A-AW!!!

Suddenly there had arisen the most unearthly clamour that Alice had ever heard.

The bell-horse stumbled and fell, and as she floated gently to the ground, Alice thought she heard Johnny's voice—far, far away—shouting, "The Raven! The Raven! Mind the trees don't fall on you!"

"That must be the Raven that cried 'croak' and they all fell down," said Alice to herself.

"And I've only eight lives left," the Kitten murmured sadly, opening one eye, then going to sleep again immediately on Alice's shoulder. Alice was too much interested in what was happening about her to realize that this was the first time the Kitten had spoken a word.

Everything seemed to be falling. The mill had collapsed like a cardboard toy; the Miller and his daughter were both sprawling on the ground, and the trees of the forest themselves swayed, tottered and fell in a curious, noiseless way. Even the road was slowly caving in and becoming a sort of shallow gulley.

When Alice thought to look for the Raven, the great black bird was just disappearing in the distance, and she was almost sure she heard its hoarse, far-off laughter.

"I really ca'n't see that this is all such a joke," said Alice severely to nobody in particular.

"You'll have to hurry, or we'll never catch up to it," murmured the Kitten in a very sleepy voice, pointing feebly ahead, then falling asleep immediately, as before.

Alice looked and saw the big steaming dumpling rolling slowly along down the sunken road not far ahead of them. Now that most of the trees had fallen, there was more light and she could see quite a distance.

The bell-horse had disappeared; so remembering that she was very hungry and feeling, too, that the sooner they got out of the way of the ill-tempered Miller the better, Alice acted upon the White Kitten's advice and started to run as fast as she could after the rolling dumpling.

Before Alice had gone more than a dozen yards, there came the sound of running footsteps behind her, and thinking that it was surely the Miller in swift pursuit, she redoubled her speed and actually *flew*, for the road was now caving in so rapidly and Alice was bounding along at such a remarkable speed that her feet only occasionally touched the ground....

It was with great relief that Alice soon heard a familiar voice, just behind her panting, "You need not fear—'tis I, my dear." Looking back she saw the Poet, whom she had forgotten all about, with his long hair streaming out behind him. A pink riding coat—several sizes too large—which he was now wearing, flapped about his slender legs as he caught up to her with tremendous leaps.

Alice was really very glad to see him again. "After all, he *is* a good natured fellow and pleasant company, even if he *does* always talk in verse," she sud to herself.

"I too, have lost my good bell-horse—the Raven was the cause of course," said. the Poet conversationally; then noticing the dumpling—which somehow, no matter how fast they went kept just about the same distance ahead of them—he exclaimed: "I say, how lucky! As for *me*, I'm just as empty as can be. We really must increase our speed if on yon dumpling we would feed, but there's the sentry-box, my dear, and now, perhaps, the Grenadier—"

"Halt!" a tremendous voice—coming apparently from a sentry-box at the side of the road—boomed out, and the next moment a soldier, at least seven feet tall, in a brilliant scarlet and white uniform and very heavy hob-nailed shoes, stepped stiffly out. He held a musket in one hand and large pewter tankard in the other.

At the thunderous command, "Halt!" Alice and the Poet stopped short, for the huge Grenadier was really a terrifying person. The Dumpling, however, paid no attention but bounced past the sentry-box without any slackening of its speed. (Alice now noticed for the first time that the dumpling was provided

At the thunderous command "Halt!" Alice and the Poet stopped short.

with short arms and legs and was not really *rolling*, but was progressing by turning handsprings in rapid succession.)

The Grenadier scowled at it in stupid surprise and again bawled out, "Halt!" this time so loud that the tin sentry-box rocked and clattered. Then to Alice's astonishment, he laid his musket on the ground and balanced himself clumsily upon his head. Taking his musket again and placing it upside-down to his shoulder he now aimed long and carefully at the fast disappearing Dumpling.

While the Grenadier was doing this, the Poet said to Alice in a rapid whisper, "He shows by his actions *he* knows how to shoot. His idea's original, clever, and cute. A musket *will* kick as you probably know—one's often knocked over, so hard is the blow—and if one should land on one's head it's no joke: one's neck is as likely as not to be broke. *He's* wise then to stand on his head, I repeat, for when the gun kicks, he'll be knocked to his feet. Moreover—"

Here there was a deafening explosion and from the Grenadier's musket came a great puff of white smoke which instead of quickly blowing away, as smoke usually does, kept spreading and spreading and getting thicker and whiter and thicker and whiter, until finally it blotted out the sentry-box... and the fallen trees... and the road....

CHAPTER VII

The Summersault Sally

"Why, it isn't smoke at all any more!" exclaimed Alice. "It's more like clouds, and we're flying again!" And sure enough—she and the Poet *were* flying through a sky full of billowy white clouds as soft and inviting as feather beds.

The kitten had disappeared.

"Couldn't we stop and rest for awhile on one of these comfortable-looking clouds?" suggested Alice. "Perhaps the kitten is coming along behind us and would catch up."

The Poet replied very earnestly, "My child—if I may be allowed—please *never* rest upon a cloud, whatever else you do. You might, while lying there, fall fast asleep you see, and as time passed your couch might break in two. Or, as your cloud went sailing by, some mountain top or spire high might bump you black and blue. *Or* say you slumbered softly there, rocked by the west wind—I declare—a weather vane! Look! *Do.*"

The Poet pointed excitedly ahead to where a picturesque ship weather-vane had just appeared above the slowly settling clouds.

"It's *exactly* like the one on the big old house at the turn of the river below Godstow," exclaimed Alice.

The clouds, which during the last few minutes had been flattening out and settling, had changed by *now* to a rather milky-looking sea through which the weather-vane ship seemed to be sailing.

Alice, as they neared the vessel, was surprised at her size and completeness. "Why, I do believe it's a *real* ship!" she cried. "And what's that name on the stem?"

"Well," chuckled the Poet, "may I be pursued by the pump in the alley, if that's not the crazy old *Summersault Sally!*"

*   *   *   *

When they arrived on the sloping deck of the antiquated *Summersault Sally*, the first thing Alice noticed was a number of enormous white rats, in sailor suits, busily engaged in coiling up cordage. "Perhaps," she said to herself, "those ropes are the *ratlines*. But why," she asked the Poet, "should anyone want rats for sailors?"

The Poet considered a moment and then said, "Rats always

leave a sinking ship, you see, so I suppose, the Captain takes 'em every trip, for while they're 'round he knows—"

Here a rumbling voice from the forward part of the ship reached their ears and the Poet cut short his explanation of the rat sailors to say, "Ah, there's good Captain Tee Wee now—just hear him singing in the bow."

The clouds had changed by now to a rather milky-looking sea.

Looking in the direction whence the sound came, Alice saw a tiny man, hardly more than two feet high, dressed in a very exaggerated nautical costume. He was doing a curious sort of a "revolving sailor dance", and singing in a voice that might have belonged to a giant, the following song:

> *"Oh, never, never leave, my lads,*
> *Your happy, happy home.*
> *Your parents' hearts 'twill grieve, my lads,*
> *If off to sea you roam.*
> *Then listen to, polite, my lads,*
> *This ballad; hark ye well,*
> *For sure as black is white, my lads,*
> *It is the truth I tell.*
> *Young Percival O. Pink, my lads,*
> *He ran away to sea,*
> *Although you'd never think, my lads,*
> *A thing like that could be.*
> *For Percy's home, you know, my lads,*
> *Was fine as one could wish.*
> *So why then should he go, my lads,*
> *To face the flying-fish?*
> *Pink's parrot sang, they say, my lads,*
> *'The Battle of the Ford'*
> *Five hundred times a day, my lads,*
> *And Percy, he was* BORED....
> *His mother 'most went mad, my lads,*
> *When Perce could not be found.*

She says, says she, "E's went to sea,
And surely will be drowned!'
His father, Peter Pink, my lads,
Says, 'Dry your heyes, my dear,
For lookee, Peg, 'is wooden leg
Will float 'im, never fear.'
She sobbed afresh and said, my lads,
'When hoff to sea 'e chased,
That wooden limb—oh, woe is 'im—
'E LEFT IT IN 'IS 'ASTE!
Says Pete, 'Your tears you waste, my love,
'Is 'aste with 'im must be,
So if it's in 'is 'aste, my love,
'E's got it, don't you see?'
Then do the Captain's jig, my lads,
And keel and double-haul,
And lower away the gig, my lads,
And catch me if I fall!"

The diminutive Captain's whirling, bounding dance had been growing more and more energetic as the song proceeded, and with the last words, which were panted rather than sung, he bounced right into Alice, who, to keep him from falling, caught him in her arms, where for a while he lay gasping like a fish out of water.

When Captain Tee Wee had recovered his breath, Alice placed him carefully on the deck, thinking as she did so, "He looks just like a live sailor-doll."

The tiny fellow still seemed a trifle dizzy and uncertain, but after a moment he remarked casually, "Last time it was the Snipe caught me."

"Oh, is the Snipe on board?" cried Alice. "I was afraid he might have been caught and put in—er—ah—that is—" Here she broke off, for it occurred to her that it might be just as well to say nothing about the pipe and the setting afire of the King's haystack.

"Oh yes, he was caught!" thundered the Captain, who had now entirely recovered his voice. "*He* was caught all right enough, Missy, but they lets him out on bail, though I'd about as lief go to the dungeons as have to ride around on *that* there lubberly beast."

"They're looking for his accomplice now," he went on very seriously, but with a mischievous wink at the Poet. "Some say as how he was seen, at the time the haystack caught fire, with a little girl with lightish hair. About *your* age, she was, Missy, I should judge."

Here the Captain looked hard at Alice, then raised his eyebrows and slowly winked at the Poet. "They ought to be back soon," he said reflectively, after a moment.

Alice, who was beginning to feel a little anxious, was about to ask whom he meant by "they", when the ship, which had been rolling and pitching only moderately, gave a more decided lurch than usual and the poor Captain tumbled over flat on his back. Alice and the Poet had barely picked him up and set him on his feet when again he tumbled, now falling forward on his nose. As they helped him to rise he muttered peevishly, "If only I hadn't lost that key, I'd not be falling about so."

Then, after a vain search through all his pockets, he continued, "That confounded Snipe's probably carried it off, for a joke. Souse him in bilge-water! Like as not he's a using of it *now* for a sinker!"

"Please, *what* key are you talking about, and what can it *possibly* have to do with your falling down so much?" asked Alice with some impatience.

"Why, the key to my sea-chest, of course, child!" roared the Captain. "That's where I keep my sea-legs," he added, in quieter explanation. "The feet on 'em, you know, are werry much larger than *land*-feet, and the knees have springs in 'em that pulls you up straight whenever you starts to fall." As if to illustrate this point. Captain Tee Wee bent his knees and began to sway back and forth, and—the *Summersault Sally* pitching, just then, unexpectedly—down he went once more, this time rolling over and over along the deck toward an open hatchway. Just as he reached it, a man, evidently a Cook, appeared coming up through the opening carrying a very

large, full soup tureen, and into this with a great splash, fell the poor little Captain!

Evidently the soup was not very hot, for the Cook unconcernedly fished the sputtering Captain out and set him, dripping, on his feet, merely saying, respectfully, as he peered anxiously into the tureen: "I'm *werry* much afraid as 'ow most of it's spilled, sir." Here the Cook glanced meaningly at Alice and the Poet and shook his head in a discouraged sort of way, as if to say, "This sort of thing happens almost every day, you know."

"And it's probably ruined my watch," choked the Captain, mournfully, pulling from a pocket in his blouse a short length of fish-line and a very curious object, which looked more like a large brass peg-top than a watch, though Alice saw that there *was* a row of numerals painted around it up near the peg.

"You may look at it if you like, Missy," the Captain added, handing the strange watch and the fishing line to Alice. (She had started to mop him off with her small handkerchief and was having a very discouraging time of it.) "It's my *self-winding* port watch," he went on, proudly. "You see, I wind it *myself.*"

"I suppose you have to spin it with the fish-line, like a boy's top?" said Alice, smiling at the Captain's last remark.

"That's the beauty of it, Missy, that's the beauty of it," cried the Captain, enthusiastically. "You see *this* here watch only goes while you're a-spinning of it; and while it's a-spinning, you nacherly ca'n't tell time by it, Missy. Coz why? Coz you ca'n't see the numbers on it then, nohow."

"Well," said Alice, doubtfully, "I shouldn't call that a very *satisfactory* kind of time-piece."

"A very *good* one, *I* should say—to lose a train by, anyway," put in the Poet, with a grin.

"Best kind, I calls it," said the Captain very positively; "never a-proddin' of you by remindin' you it's gettin' late for something or other. Leaves all that to your own good judgement, like." He had been clumsily winding the fishing line about the watch as he spoke and now he drew back his arm to spin it. In so doing he jostled the Cook, who during the conversation had been standing behind him thoughtfully drinking up what was left of the soup. The tureen dropped from the Cook's hands, but instead of breaking into a thousand pieces on the deck—as might have been expected—it *bounced* like a large rubber ball!

Alice, who had been sitting on the ship's low rail, reached out wildly in an attempt to catch the tureen as it bounced over the side....

C H A P T E R V I I I

Buttermilk Channel

Milkman! Milkman! Where have you been?
In Buttermilk Channel up to my chin.
I spilt my milk; I spoiled my clothes—
And got a long icicle hung to my nose.

The next thing Alice knew, she was floundering about in a sea of buttermilk!

The buttermilk, curiously enough, did not seem to wet or chill her, though, as she discovered later it was deliciously cool to drink.

When she had recovered her wits sufficiently to look about her, Alice saw that the *Summersault Sally* was already some distance away and plunging along at great speed. She could just make out the familiar figure of the Poet leaning far out over the rail, waving his hand; and, carried on the breeze, came the words, "So sorry that you have to leave. Goodbye! Give my regards to

Steve." The next moment the ship had disappeared in a bank of fog.

After swimming about aimlessly for a time, Alice found to her surprise that she could touch bottom with her feet and still keep her head and shoulders above the surface. This, of course, was a great relief, but it was very tedious just standing about in this way with nothing in sight but buttermilk and not a soul to converse with. So after a while Alice began talking aloud to herself as she usually did when all alone. "Well, of all the uninteresting, lonesome situations, this is the very worst. I *do* wish some one would come.

"And I wonder who 'Steve' is?" she continued after a moment or two, remembering the Poet's farewell words: "I daresay I shall meet him before long anyway."

"Werry probably, Miss, werry probably, coz *Long* ca'n't be found nowhere," said a melancholy voice startlingly close behind her.

Alice turned in such haste that she lost her footing on the slippery bottom and went under.

When she came up again, sputtering, the little girl saw this rather curious sight—a large dented milk can balanced on the head of a very sad-faced undersized man who was standing almost up to his neck in the buttermilk. A long icicle hanging from the end of his nose helped to make his expression almost ludicrously woebegone.

"And wot's more," he was

now continuing dolefully, apparently not having taken the slightest notice of Alice's mishap. "I'm Steve! Steve for short—that is, Steven Short's me 'ole name, Miss. Long 'e *was* my pardner and that, as you might say, is the Long and Short of it. But, as I were a-sayin' afore, 'e 'asn't been seen for days, Miss."

"How did he happen to get lost?" asked Alice, feeling that it was time for her to make some sort of remark.

"It's a sad story, a most distressin' story, that it is—(here the Milkman's voice almost broke). You see, Miss, my pardner Long were an uncommon *tall* man, a regiler giant he were, and hunfor-tunately 'is heyesight were werry poor. And it's probable that 'is heyes gettin' poor—and 'im bein' so tall—'e finally got so's 'e couldn't see no further than 'is knees, Miss, and 'is feet they took 'im hup the wrong road somewheres. Leastways that's my hopinion."

"How very unfortunate," was all Alice could think of to say in consolation, and the Milkman after sighing deeply went on: "That ain't my wust trouble, Miss, not by no means; Moolygeezer—that's my cow—she went plumb crazy, Miss— what with jumpin' hover the moon—and I ca'n't never catch 'er no more at milkin' time. So I 'as to keep goats now (here he choked back a sob) and sell buttermilk."

"I never knew that goats gave *buttermilk*," said Alice rather timidly.

"*My* goats, you see, Miss, are all butters," groaned the Milkman so dismally that Alice hastened to change the subject.

"Please," she enquired, "*why* do you carry that big milk can balanced on your *head*? It must be *very* tiring."

"Well, Miss," answered the Milkman thoughtfully, "there's several reasons: It makes me look a bit taller, fer one thing, and then too, it pertects my 'ead where the 'air's gettin' scarce, as you might say. I lost my 'at, Miss, when I hups an' slips hoffen the hiceberg, and I'll probably never set heyes on that 'at again."

Here the poor little Milkman began to weep openly, most of the tears running down his long nose and thence down the icicle which hung from the end of it. "I suppose," thought Alice, who always liked to find good reasons for everything, "that's how the icicle was formed. It must have been the freezing cold on that iceberg and every time he cried the tears ran down his nose and froze."

The Milkman continued sobbing quietly, only stopping now and then to say in a choking voice, "It's all been werry depressing for me, werry depressing indeed."

Alice racked her brain to discover some way to divert his mind from his many troubles, and finally unable to think of any consoling or amusing remarks of her own, she decided in desperation to simply recite the first thing that came into her head; this happened to be *"Down by the River"*. It went along quite correctly for a line or two, but changed very queerly after that, and this was the result:

> *I was walking by the river,*
> *One spring morning long ago,*
> *And the reeds were all aquiver;*
> *(They're such NERVOUS things you know);*
> *I had paused a while to listen*
> *To the singing of the stream,*
> *When a voice said, "Now it isn't*
> *My desire to make you scream,*
> *Or alarm you, ma'am, unduly,*
> *But if I were YOU, I'd run,*
> *For you're in great danger, truly,*
> *And you haven't got a gun!"*
> *This surprising voice of warning*
> *Came, I noticed from a bird*

On a tree-top: "Just this morning,"
It continued, "I have heard
A voracious Tigerilla
Growling 'round this very tree.
MY advice is—seek your villa!
Why, from HERE I PLAINLY see
Seven Fryingpanthers stealthy
Coming hot upon your trail,
And you know they're MOST unhealthy,
'Less you catch 'em by the tail.
So, you see, you'd better scramble.
Though there's hardly any hope,
For, approaching at an amble,
Comes an Elephantelope!"
These were words to make one worry.
I stood shivering with dread—
And was just about to scurry,
When a catfish calmly said,
"Nothing's coming to pursue you;
Ma'am, don't you believe a word,
For that fellow talking to you
Is the far-famed LYRE bird!"

Although Alice's verse did not seem to have had a very noticeably cheering effect on the Milkman, he had at any rate ceased sobbing and the tears were no longer running off the end of his nose.

"Medium good, medium," he murmured gloomily, after quite a long pause. "But just listen to *these* here werses," he added more brightly and drew a soggy, dripping sheet of familiar crimson paper from his breast pocket (the tide was evidently ebbing, for the second button of the Milkman's coat was now visible); "the Poet he wrote it special for me, for to pay my milk bill; you see, Miss, 'e—"

"Oh, do *you* know the Poet too?" interrupted Alice. "He's really quite a friend of mine." It somehow seemed to her that she had known the Poet for a very long time.

"I knowed 'im *last week*, Miss, but, my Gallons! 'e 'as that many disguises that you ca'n't always rightly tell 'o's 'im, as you might say. I knows 'im when 'e's a scarecrow, an' I knows 'im when 'e's a weal-an'-'am pie, and they do say 'e's *wonderful* convincin' as a signpost," he added earnestly, handing Alice the dripping sheet (he had been clum-  sily attempting to dry it by rubbing it with his coat-sleeve which was if possible even wetter than the paper). "You'd better read it to yourself, Miss, hafter all," he said huskily. "You see, it's really *too* haffectin' to me; not only for its hown sake, as you might say, but for the sake o' the six bob 'e never paid me."

Fearing that the Milkman would burst into tears again, Alice took the sheet. She could just manage to make out the blurred writing, and this is what she read:—

YEARNINGS
For years and years I've peddled Milk,
From Trent to Timbuktu,
And also cream, though 'twas my dream
Far different things to do.
Far different things to do, to do,
Far finer things to do!

For instance, I should like to drive,
Around and round the square,
A pink and purple omnibus,
How people all would stare!

Or, think how pleasant it would be
To stand for hours and hours,
Upon some snow-capped mountain-peak
A-selling paper flowers.
Then one might fish for griddle-cakes
Each night twixt twelve and two:
I sob and sigh, to think that I
So many things don't do.
I'd take soft soap and seashore sand,
And mix 'em up with tea,
And of them make a cobble cake,
To sell at 1 and 3.
My sweetest dream of all is this—
(I love a change of scene)
At the North Pole, to dig a hole,
And plant a Lima bean;
And plant a Lima bean, a bean,
A lovely Lima bean!

While she was reading, Alice had noticed that the buttermilk they were standing in was gradually thinning and changing to clear water. She was just about to call the Milkman's attention to this when she suddenly heard the sharp rub-a-dub-dubbing of a drum behind her. Looking in the direction from whence the sound came, Alice beheld a most amusing spectacle.

A stiff breeze had sprung up and a huge tub was approaching, spinning round and round and bobbing up and down on the choppy waves. In the tub were three men, a Butcher and a Baker—easily recognizable by their dress-and a third occupant, whom Alice, because of his very insignificant size, did not notice at first.

The Baker had tried to rig up a sail by tying his apron to a long French loaf and was making desperate efforts to brace the strange mast with his knees and hold the flapping ends of the apron at the same time. At his wild contortions even the melancholy Milkman smiled feebly.

The Butcher, his face purple with exertion, was paddling as best he could with a large meat-cleaver; the only result of this was, of course, to keep the tub spinning faster and faster and make the work of holding up the mast all the harder for the poor Baker.

As the strange craft drew nearer, Alice saw a tiny fellow—even smaller than Captain Tee Wee—standing in it, furiously busy beating a drum almost as big as himself. He was apparently wholly oblivious to his surroundings.

"I've never seen so many dwarfish people as there are in this queer country," thought Alice. "Perhaps it's because the Artist wasn't as careful as he should have been in drawing some of them."

So intent were the occupants of the tub upon what they were doing that Alice and her companion attracted no notice at all from them until a shrill whistle and a surprisingly loud "Milk

A huge tub was approaching, spinning round and round.

Ooooo-h!" from the Milkman caused them to cease their frantic efforts.

"Lard-a-pork!" shouted the Butcher (merely a Butcher's way of saying "Hard-a-port") after a moment's panting pause, and then steering with his cleaver he brought the spinning craft about so sharply that it bumped heavily into the poor Milkman, knocking the milk can off his head. The cover of the can came off and the milk spilled into the tub, knocking over and nearly drowning the little man with the drum.

"Oh, dear! We *beg* your pardon," began Alice—for somehow or other she felt responsible for the mishap. "We really didn't mean—"

She was interrupted in her apologies by a loud, joyful shout of "Dinner Time!" from the Baker, who was already breaking up the long French loaf he had been using as a mast and throwing the pieces into the milk which was swashing about in the now almost submerged tub.

Chapter IX

Tub and Tunnel

Alice soon found herself sitting on the edge of the tub with the others, who were all now eating in ravenous silence. On one side of her sat the Milkman, who was having a very hard time to keep his own equilibrium on the unstable seat and at the same time balance the now empty can which he had again placed on his head.

On the other side sat the tiny fellow with the drum which he was now using with great success as a bowl for the bread and milk. Having this advantage over the others, who were forced to scoop it up with their hands, he finished his meal first.

Poor Alice, on the other hand, although very hungry, had been unable to get any of the food, for every time she reached down to scoop it up she nearly lost her balance, and besides, the tub seemed always to roll in such a way as to keep the bread and milk just out of her reach. So after a while she gave up the attempt altogether and turned to look at the dwarfish being beside her.

Alice now noticed for the first time that he wore a curious shiny yellow hat (exactly like a small, brass candle-holder), on top of which was a short stub of candle. From an inside pocket of his long, tightly buttoned yellow "duster" he now drew forth a large card with a deep black border:—

> ## JOE SMITH 36 + 4–7 M. M.
>
> CANDLESTICKS
> EXECUTED
> AND
> REPAIRED

This card he handed to Alice with quite a flourish.

"Why," she exclaimed, "I thought you were a drummer! Although," she added, "I might have known that the Candlestick-maker went about with the Butcher and the Baker."

"You see," said the little man ("with really quite a 'high society' air," as Alice said afterward), "candlestick making is nice *light* work for one of my size—I'm a trifle small, as you may possibly have noticed, my dear. The Butcher and Baker are old neighbours of mine," he went on, "and we always take our holidays together."

"As to the drum, I learned to play to please Pansy—Pansy is very musical, oh, *very* musical, indeed," and, pointing to the letters "M. M." after his name on the card Alice was holding, he continued: "You see I'm a married man—clever abbreviation that—rather impressive, too—and avoids all confusion, eh?"

"But what are the numbers on the card for, and the mourning border?" asked Alice, feeling that she ought to show a proper amount of interest.

"The numbers give my age," beamed the Candlestick-maker triumphantly; "that is, if you're good at figures. *Two and twenty* is the answer, I believe, if you work it out *carefully*."

"*I* make it *three and thirty*," Alice ventured rather timidly, for nothing seemed really dependable any more, not even the rules of arithmetic.

"Possibly you're right, my dear, possibly you're right," answered the Candlestick-maker hastily. "You know yourself how time flies, eh?"

Then after a moment's pause he added solemnly, "The mourning band is for the candlesticks I have to *execute*—I never *did* like that part of the business. Why, once—but *do* let's talk of something else, my dear; that's not at all a cheerful subject for an after-dinner conversation. I say, *are* you good at telling stories? There's nothing *like* a good exciting yarn after dinner, eh?"

Alice *intended* to reply that she could think of no really exciting story at the moment, but upon opening her mouth to do so, she was astonished to hear herself reciting, with appropriate gestures, the following verses:

THE VILLAGE CHOIR

Oh, the fire-bell was ringing
  In the town of Ballyhack,
And the village choir was singing,
  "Bring, oh, bring my Benny back."
Now a simple, soothing story
  Is this tale of Shanghaied Ben,
Just, perhaps, a bit too gory
  Where his ears are clipped, but then
There's a fairly happy ending,
  Though the tune is mostly glum.
(As a rule it's quite heart-rending
  On the fog-horn and the drum.)
Well—the songing and the singing
  'Bout the bringing back of Ben,
And the donging and the dinging
  Mingled sweetly; so that when
The Policeman—who was taking
  Of his after-dinner snooze—
Heard it, he, instead of waking,
  Dreamed he read the "Oxford News"!

During the recital of Alice's verses the Butcher, the Baker, and the melancholy Milkman, who had finally finished eating the last of the bread and milk, had all been yawning audibly—which was of course *very* rude under the circumstances—and seemed to be having an increasingly difficult time to keep awake and to preserve their balance on the rim of the tub. Just as she came to the last word, they all tumbled overboard very neatly and quietly, and floated off, bobbing up and down like corks on the green water, all three snoring in perfect unison. :They do it precisely as though they had practised it together a great many times," thought Alice.

The little Candlestick-maker held his sides and rocked back and forth so alarmingly that Alice feared he, too, would fall overboard.

"It was either that part about the 'after-dinner' snooze or the last line about reading the '*Oxford News*' that finished 'em," he managed to say when he could control his shrill laughter.

"It was *very* unmannerly of them at any rate," said Alice, "but shouldn't we try to get them aboard again?" She felt vaguely that something ought to be done, though as a matter of fact all three of the floating sleepers looked perfectly comfortable and happy where they were.

"I make it a rule," said the Candlestick-maker seriously, "*never* to disturb a man when he's taking his after-dinner nap. He's apt to wake up very cross. Besides, it'll help their digestions to sleep a bit. And speaking of digestions," he rattled on, "reminds me of cheese, and cheese reminds me of cake (here he reached toward the pocket of his yellow coat). Now what would you say to a piece?"

"Oh," answered Alice, in delighted anticipation, "I'd say 'thank you, very much'; there's *nothing* I like better, especially *pound* cake!"

"Well, I'd hardly say all *that* to a piece of cake I'd never met before," said the Candlestick-maker reprovingly. "However, it doesn't really matter, for I wasn't referring to a piece of cake anyhow; only to a piece of *poetry*. It's my turn, you know," he added with a chuckle, apparently enjoying his little joke immensely.

Alice sat back with a long sigh of resignation.

These repeated disappointments in the matter of food were becoming most aggravating. "I wonder," she said to herself wistfully, "if I shall ever really get anything to eat again?"

The Candlestick-maker now drew from his pocket a folded sheet of yellow paper which he smoothed out and dusted carefully on both sides with his tiny handkerchief. He then handed it to Alice, remarking with a pleasant smile, "Perhaps you'd rather read it yourself, eh? It's really *most* appropriate to this occasion, my dear." Then without waiting for a reply he cleared his throat complacently once or twice and, taking the paper out of Alice's hand, before she had had time to more than glance at the first line, he read with great satisfaction:

A MATTER OF TASTE
What kind of food do I prefer?
My tastes are simple, QUITE!
I like the pickled chestnut burr,
And now and then a bite
Of sugared oleander bark
And, in the early spring,
Green cactus, gathered after dark
On Tuesday, is the thing!
Some claim that kerosene and sand,
Though ticklish to the tongue,
Beats even frozen fritters and
Is fine for old and young.

A friend of mine once used to make
A stew of lizard legs
And linseed oil; while jelly cake
He'd salt away in kegs.
Of course, we ca'n't be all alike

In what we choose to chew—
A fine purée of railroad spike
Might not appeal to YOU.
But that reminds me. Uncle Ben,
To ask you, what's YOUR choice.
What victuals do YOU call for when
Your appetite you voice?
Do you demand wild roses panned—
Or choc'late-coated eels?
Unc' scratched his head then slowly said,
"What I like most is—meals!"

As any reference to food was becoming very painful to Alice, she made no comment on this doggerel, and, in the interval of silence that followed, the Candlestick-maker, with the injured air of one whose best efforts have been unappreciated, carefully folded the sheet, sealed it with a bright yellow wafer which he had taken from a pocket of his coat, affixed a stamp with elaborate care and then, taking a stubby pencil from behind his ear, he hastily printed *"IMPORTANT! PLEASE*

RUSH" across the back of the folded paper and threw it into the water.

The silence finally became so depressing to Alice that she decided to introduce a new subject for conversation; so, pointing to a large "FOR SALE" tag which was tied to one of the handles of the tub, she asked very politely, "Is this boat of yours really for sale, please, or is that only its name?"

"It may be for *sale,*" answered the Candlestick-maker, without looking up (he was now gloomily trying to shine his wet shoes with the ends of his yellow necktie). "It may be for *sale,*" he repeated bitterly, "but as it hasn't even a foresail, *certainly* wasn't made for *sailing!* He seemed quite pleasantly surprised at his own feeble joke and, much to Alice's relief, recovered his good humour immediately and began vigorously beating his flabby little drum, finally placing it on the floor and dancing a *"Baccy Pipes"* jig upon the drum head.

The jarring of this dancing loosened some of the staves of the tub and Alice saw that leaks were starting in a dozen places.

"Do leave off," she cried anxiously. "You'll sink us, I'm sure!"

The Candlestick-maker stopped his jigging abruptly and selecting the worst leak, tried to stop it; first with his tiny handkerchief and then by lying along the crack through which the water was pouring in quite a torrent. Of course, this did no good whatever. After trying vainly, in several other ridiculous ways, to stop the increasing leaks he finally shouted in a dramatic voice, "All hands stand by to man the boats!"

"But there aren't any boats," said Alice, smiling in spite of her anxiety and feeling quite proud of her own calmness.

"Well, women and children first *anyhow,* then!" cried the Candlestick-maker, who seemed to be thoroughly enjoying the excitement of sinking.

Alice had prepared herself for the worst (the tub was filling fast and seemed about to take the final plunge) when, with a very gentle scraping bump, they struck bottom in about eight inches of water.

"Must be low tide," muttered the Candlestick-maker in a disappointed voice. "Of course, it's all right, I suppose, for the sea to be *tidey*, but there is such a thing as carrying it too far, *I* say. Just as we were going down so famously, too."

"Well," said Alice, "I'm rather glad we went aground, on the whole."

"But we *didn't* go aground on any hole, for *that ca'n't be done*, you know," said the Candlestick-maker very positively and impressively, as if stating some surprisingly unusual fact.

"I meant on the '*W*-H-O-L-E', not on the '*H*-O-L-E', of course," retorted Alice, somewhat annoyed by the little man's air of superior wisdom.

"Well, since you're so *sure* of it perhaps we *had* better take a look at any rate," said the Candlestick-maker, in a conciliatory manner, adding hopefully, as he peered over the side, "It may be only a *half*, you know."

Alice now saw that in the sparkling clear water were a great many goldfish, who seemed to be having a sort of pursuit-race round and round the tub. Besides the goldfish there were many other aquatic creatures of different sorts and sizes— most of them watching the race—and a little apart from the rest Alice noticed a group of three or four very brown, fried oysters talking earnestly together.

Upon catching sight of these, the Candlestick-maker exclaimed, "My Eye, but aren't they tanned! *They* must have lived in the tropics a long time. By the way, you don't happen to have any oyster crackers with you, I suppose? We could—"

He was interrupted by the familiar shrill sound of a postman's whistle. A rather large fish was approaching, carrying a leather mail bag. As he drew near Alice saw that he wore a neat little grey, visored cap upon which was lettered neatly, POSTMAN.

He seemed to be in a great hurry, as postmen usually are. Taking a rather bulky package from his bag he tossed it to Alice, remarking pleasantly, "Proper fine day, Miss;" then, touching his cap, he was off.

"Nothing for me?" the Candlestick-maker called after him. But the Postman kept on, unheeding, and soon disappeared from view.

"It's high time I was getting an answer," said the little man, complainingly.

"But who *do* you suppose sent me *this*?" Alice exclaimed, surprised and delighted at receiving this unexpected piece of mail.

"Probably it's only a note from the Stage Manager, reminding you to be on time for the rehearsal," said the Candlestick-maker, trying hard to keep the envy out of his voice. "Though, of course after all this delay we're frightfully late, already."

Although she had not the slightest idea what "rehearsal" her little companion was referring to, Alice did not ask for particulars just then. She was too much occupied with her fascinating mail package. It was a most interesting looking one, too; wrapped in oiled silk and tied with a piece of seaweed. Furthermore, the packet was rather heavy for its size and almost completely covered with two-penny stamps except for the small space where ALICE M. was written in green ink.

"What does the M stand for?" asked the Candlestick-maker rather suspiciously. "You see," he went on before giving her time to reply, "it *might* mean ALICE *MAYBE*! So perhaps it's not for you after all. It *might* even be intended for me."

This was a rather disturbing thought, especially as, curiously enough, Alice could not for the life of her, at the moment, remember her full name. "It stands—" she said, hesitating uncertainly as she started to open the package, "I *think* it stands for my last name."

"Your *last* name, eh? How often do you change your name, I'd like to know? And you ca'n't even be sure what the last one was! I suppose ALICE is the name you had before you changed it for this last one that you ca'n't remember. Well, there's something mighty suspicious about it, that's all *I* can say."

Poor Alice was so confused by this rapid and complicated speech, that she did not even try to argue about the name but said weakly, "I suppose so," and went on unwrapping her package, which proved to contain a small collapsible telescope and a thin pack of little red cards, tied together with a broad white ribbon upon which were printed the letters "S. C. T.". Upon each of the cards was written a single word. Alice read them off just as they happened to come in the little pack.

LOOK YOURS BEEN P. SEE TRULY SPYGLASS THROUGH THAT THE YOU'LL WE'VE AND WRECKED.

"No doubt it means *something*," said Alice, half aloud, after she had tried many different combinations of the words without success.

"Maybe it's some sort of a cipher message," said the Candlestick-maker, eagerly. He seemed to have entirely forgotten his suspicions and had been looking through the large end of the pocket telescope with great intentness; now at Alice and not out to where the Butcher, the Baker and the Milkman were just disappearing on the horizon. He now handed the glass to Alice and taking the cards examined them carefully one by one. "Of course, that P. means that it's a message from the Poet!" he cried excitedly, after a moment or two. "And he almost *always* uses a secret code." Then, taking from his pocket a little yellow-covered book, he started rapidly thumbing over the pages, all of which seemed to be covered with row after row of zeros. "Here it is!" the Candlestick-maker finally cried delightedly. "The 'S. C. T.' on the ribbon means 'SHUFFLE CARDS TWICE'!" Then in his excitement, instead of putting the book back in his pocket, he threw it into the water where it was immediately swallowed by a fat, sleepy looking fish labelled "LIBRARIAN".

"You shuffle 'em once, and then *I'll* shuffle 'em once," he suggested eagerly. They did this and the cards then read:

LOOK THROUGH THE SPY-GLASS AND YOU'LL SEE THAT WE'VE BEEN WRECKED.

YOURS TRULY,

P.

"How exciting!" cried Alice. "And what fun that puzzle was. But I do hope none of them was drowned." And then, shutting one eye, she raised the spy-glass to the other....

Alice found to her astonishment that she was not looking through a telescope at all, but was standing in a dark, narrow railroad tunnel.

The opening at the end of the tunnel seemed miles ahead, and yet as Alice looked at the circle of light she began to see what looked at first like a rather blurry magic-lantern picture of a "Storm at Sea".

As the picture grew clearer, she made out, in the foreground, a number of rats swimming through the waves in two very straight lines, like soldiers, with one especially large rat, who seemed to be a sort of Colonel, in the lead. A little behind these came the Poet, the Cook, and the Captain, apparently engaged in an animated conversation. Back of this group were the Butcher, the Baker, and the Milkman, all three still sleeping heavily. Bringing up the rear of this curious procession was a tremendous turtle floundering doggedly along.

Alice laughed heartily at the strangely ridiculous picture. "If only they had a fife and drum it would be a regular 'aquatic parade'," she chuckled. "I'm sure I wish—" She was interrupted at this point by the scraping splutter of a match just back of her, and turning saw that it was the Candlestick-maker whom, of course, she had not noticed in the darkness of the tunnel. He was lighting the short candle on top of his hat; this done, he drew from his pocket (which seemed to be inexhaustible) a small fife and, handing it to Alice, remarked: "Not bad, that idea of yours about the fife and drum music, my dear. Fancy what a tremendous, *beautiful* noise it'll make in this tunnel, too!" he went on enthusiastically. "We might try *'Soldiers of the Queen'* first, eh?"

Now Alice had never before even *tried* to play a fife, so she was more than a little surprised to find upon attempting it very doubtfully, that she could play with considerable ease and flourish.

The Candlestick-maker adjusted his drum and they marched along up the track, the tunnel reverberating with the din of their fifing and drumming.

Alice was so occupied with her delightful new-found accomplishment that for a time she forgot the strange procession of swimmers; and when after finishing *"Soldiers of the Queen"* she looked for it again, it had changed to merely a blank spot of bright light such as one always sees at the end of a tunnel.

They were about to start on another lively tune when the Candlestick-maker, pointing excitedly, shouted: "Here's luck!" And the dim light thrown by the candle revealed a small hand-car standing motionless just ahead of them on the track. It proved to be beautifully finished in mahogany and gold with soft, blue cushions upon the little platform.

"How jolly!" exclaimed Alice (the child had always longed to ride on one of these cunning little cars). And running forward she scrambled aboard and then, after helping her tiny companion up to the platform beside her, started to work the propelling handles up and down.

Away they went, very slowly at first, but steadily gaining momentum until they were finally going at a very respectable speed, though strangely enough this did not seem to get them any nearer the mouth of the tunnel. The Candlestick-maker, who was of course too small to help much with the handles, was enjoying the ride immensely; he kept saying complacently over and over, "If Pansy could only see me now, eh? If she only *could!*"

Ever since they had finished playing *"Soldiers of the Queen"* Alice had heard a muffled sound of low rumbling and whistling, which she had at first supposed to be merely the re-echoing of their drumming and fifing in the narrow tunnel;

but instead of diminishing it was now growing louder and louder and beginning to resemble more and more alarmingly the sound of a railroad engine. Looking back over her shoulder, Alice saw to her dismay that it *was* an engine, still some distance behind them to be sure, but gaining fast. She redoubled her efforts, working the propelling handles up and down frantically in her terror, and the hand-car fairly flew along the track. Their speed being now just about that of the engine, the distance between them remained for a while undiminished.

"Perhaps we wo'n't have a collision after all!" Alice shouted pantingly. The din in the tunnel was now terrific.

"I'm afraid not!" shrieked the Candlestick-maker in reply. He seemed to be deriving even more pleasure from this form of dangerous adventure than he had from the threatened sinking of the tub, and in spite of her anxiety and exertions Alice could not help smiling a little when he extracted from his wonderful pocket a large onion, a baby's nursing bottle, the kind with a long rubber tube, and a dictionary, and hurled them one after another at the approaching railroad engine.

This seemed to afford the little man huge enjoyment. As he threw the dictionary he panted happily, "If *that* ever strikes between the ears it'll do the work! It's just *full* of heavy words!"

Always ready to argue and feeling besides that a little conversation might stiffen her courage a bit, Alice shouted: "But engines haven't any ears, you know!"

"What?" shrieked the Candlestick-maker. "Do you mean to say you never saw an *engineer*?" And then completely overcome with appreciation of his own little joke he rolled about on the platform of the swaying hand-car, holding his sides and fairly choking with merriment. His drum, breaking from its strap as he rolled about, went bouncing off onto the track in front of the oncoming engine. The candle went out—and—BOOM!!! There was a terrific explosion and the car, with Alice clinging desperately to it, shot out of the dark tunnel into brilliant sunlight.

CHAPTER X

Iceberg

The speed at which they went tearing along was at first so great that Alice could make out nothing but a blur of dazzling light. The hand-car soon slowed down, however, and she saw that they were approaching a neat little station at the end of a long dock, which ran out into the ocean. The waves were running very high, although the sun was shining brightly, and the tiny station, which was built entirely of ice-blocks, was dripping with sparkling spray from the breakers.

The name of the station—"ICEBERG"—was lettered on a board which hung from the icicle-fringed eaves.

Alice felt much relieved when the hand-car came to a gentle stop at the station platform, for she had noticed that the track just beyond simply ran off the end of the dock and down into the water. She alighted hastily and then remembering the Candlestick-maker—whom she had entirely forgotten in the excitement of the last few minutes—she turned to help him off. He had vanished, leaving only his curious hat behind!

Alice now saw that the hat was, in fact, simply an average sized brass candlestick of this sort:—

Saying to herself, "I'll just keep this as a memento," she picked it up and was just starting for the door of the station when a bell jangled loudly and a voice cried, "All aboard!" and the hand-car, starting with a jerk, ran down the few remaining yards of track into the sea and disappeared.

"Well, of all the strange railroads—" Alice began, but just then she caught sight of a very white face with large coal black eyes, a pointed red nose, and a scrubby stiff goatee: it was staring at her from a small window in the station.

For a moment Alice was really frightened at this strange apparition, but it suddenly occurred to her that of course this was only a Snowman and that the carroty red nose *was* a carrot, the black eyes lumps of coal, and the goatee a worn-out paint brush. "And he really has a very kindly expression in spite of his unusual features," thought the little girl.

It somehow did not surprise her much now to hear him ask pleasantly, "Any baggage, Miss?" his paint-brush goatee wagging stiffly as he spoke.

"Nothing but this," answered Alice, holding up the candlestick and noting as she did so that the candle was again burning.

The sight of the candle apparently made the Snowman quite nervous, for he said rather shakily, "You might just blow that out, Miss, if you don't mind; I ca'n't abide a flame of *any* sort, not since my brother almost died of a bonfire."

Alice blew out the candle and the Snowman, who seemed greatly relieved, continued politely, "Just leave your bundle in the baggage room if you like." He pointed with a very short fat arm to a large clumsily-wrapped package, which Alice had certainly not seen before, standing just beside her on the platform. She was about to tell the station agent (for that was what the Snowman evidently was) that it did not belong to her, when she noticed tied to the bundle a large tag upon which was printed in bold letters—YOURS.

"But," said Alice to herself, but half aloud—really hoping that the interesting package might prove to belong to her— "How do *I* know that the tag doesn't mean that it belongs to the Snowman?"

The Snowman heard her question. "Why, Miss," he said slowly, like a good-natured teacher patiently explaining something to a stupid child, "you see, if it were *mine*, it would be marked *MINE*, but as it isn't marked *MINE* why then of course it isn't *mine: but*, if, on the other hand, it were *yours*, Miss, then it would be marked YOURS, and as it *is* marked YOURS, why then of course it *is* yours and *not* mine. Or, to put it another way," he went on triumphantly, after taking a breath, "if it were not yours—" (here he stopped, for Alice was no longer listening, but was already unwrapping the bundle, for, like most of us, she was always easily convinced of what she wanted to believe).

First came several layers of newspapers—most of them the *Gloucester Gazette* and the *Norwich News*—then straw tied round and round with heavy cord like the winter covering for a rose bush; next came a ragged old quilt decorated with a design of cabbage-like scarlet flowers. As the air was now very chilly in spite of the bright sunshine, Alice stopped to drape this quilt about her shoulders like a sort of cape. She then removed the remaining wrappings from the bundle, consisting of a fish net and several more newspapers (these being mostly *Bunbury Bugles*).

"Well of all pre-pos-terous things!" exclaimed Alice as she finally pulled off the last of the papers; for, after all her trouble in undoing the great package, its contents proved to be only a rickety old bottomless bird cage upon the little padlocked door of which hung a card bearing the words, "GONE FOR THE DAY".

The Snowman, his head and shoulders craned as far as possible out of the station window, had been watching with great interest the unwrapping of the mysterious bundle, and he now exclaimed with a chuckle which nearly dislodged his paintbrush goatee: "*Very interesting* luggage, Miss, and also *very* instructive. However," he added more seriously, "you might just hang it on that hook by the door there. (Alice was about to throw the battered cage into the sea.) You never can tell when that sort of thing will come in handy, Miss."

"You might be able to use that card on it some day when you go off for a holiday," suggested Alice, smiling in spite of her disappointment at the idea of a bottomless bird cage like this one ever "coming in handy".

"I'm afraid I'll never be going on a holiday, Miss," said the Snowman sadly. "You see, whoever it was made me, he didn't give me any legs to speak of; though I don't complain, as very few snowmen has 'em, and furthermore, Miss, it saves me lots of steps. I'm what you might call," he went on more brightly, "a *stationary* station agent, or perhaps—"

At this juncture Alice heard a sound of joyful squeaking and shrill cheering at the end of the dock and, turning, saw that the hand-car had emerged from the water and was coming back toward the station. It was swarming with the Sailor Rats, who were waving their dripping caps and generally behaving like a crowd of school boys off for a holiday.

The car did not stop at the station but kept on at steadily increasing speed, and the shrill cries soon died away in the distance.

"Those must be the Sailors from the *Summersault Sally*," exclaimed Alice, remembering the dissolving magic-lantern view she had seen in the tunnel, "and the others must be close behind, I'm sure. Rats are always the first to leave a sinking ship, at least so the Poet said."

"It's just as well those sailors didn't stop off here," said the Snowman decidedly; "they're always a rough, noisy lot, Miss, and like as not they'd have stolen the station sign and—"

"Why, *here* are the others, now!" cried Alice. While the Snowman was speaking she had spied four familiar heads on the crest of an oncoming wave. The wave broke, depositing the Poet, Captain Tee Wee, the Cook, and the Milkman in a neat row at the extreme end of the dock.

The Milkman, after looking sadly about in a bewildered way for a moment or two—apparently but half awakened by the slight shock of landing—settled back against a convenient post, closed his melancholy eyes and started snoring at once.

The others rose unconcernedly to their feet and shook themselves like three water spaniels, and Alice now heard the Cook, who seemed to be continuing an interrupted conversation, remark: "—and what I says is, it's good riddance to 'em! If them two lubbers an' that old shell-back wanted to sail with that tow 'eaded softy. Captain Shafto, why shouldn't they, *I* says, an' werry good, too."

"Right you are, matey!" roared Captain Tee Wee so heartily that several icicles fell jingling from the station eaves.

The Poet, who had just caught sight of Alice, showed no surprise whatever; he merely smiled pleasantly as if he had naturally expected her to be there, and remarked casually, jerking his thumb at his companions, "They refer to the Butcher, the Baker, and Turtle, who were taken aboard the *Meandering Myrtle*."

"But I don't remember seeing a *turtle* aboard the *Summersault Sally*," said Alice. "Where did *he* come from?"

"The waves they ran so high, you see, *our ship turned turtle*. Pardon me if I now leave you for a while to give my new disguise a trial." Thus saying, the Poet stepped into the little station, from the door of which, after but a few moments, hopped a very large, black and white penguin.

Startled by this sudden transformation, Alice took a step backward and, tripping over the trailing end of the bed quilt which she had wrapped about her, fell flat.

The penguin helped her up clumsily, remarking as he did so, "There's no need to feel such a shock of alarm: I'm only the Poet who'll do you no harm."

When Alice got to her feet again the Snowman, Captain Tee Wee, the Cook and the sleeping Milkman were gone—though she was quite sure she still heard muffled snoring. The station itself had disappeared, too, and she and the ridiculously disguised Poet were standing on what seemed at first to be the flat, icy roof of a high tower of some sort. The end of a ladder

("It looks just like the railroad track stood up on end," thought Alice) showed above a low parapet which bordered the roof.

The snoring soon changed to a sound like that of surf far below them, and peering over the parapet Alice saw, to her astonishment and dismay, that they were on the very highest pinnacle of a tremendous iceberg!

Owing to a heavy fog which surrounded the base of the iceberg, it was impossible to see where the ladder led to. "It probably rests on the bottom of the sea, and I'm sure I should never dare to climb down anyway," thought Alice miserably,

adding half aloud: "Oh, dear, I wish I had never come." Then it occurred to her that she had had nothing to do with *coming*: in fact she had not *come* at *all*. This was a very confusing thought. She felt, though, that the Poet was somehow or other to blame for their predicament; so, turning to him, she said piteously, "Whatever *shall* we do?"

Patting her shoulder with one of his ridiculous flipper-like wings, the Poet answered reassuringly: "Don't fret yourself, be calm, my dear; *I'm* really rather glad we're here. An iceberg's safe—if gales don't rise—and how it suits my new disguise! Still if you're feeling timid—well, you just might try your fire-bell."

"My *fire-bell*? I *haven't* any fire-bell and you know it," said Alice crossly; for she felt that the Poet had chosen a very poor time for teasing her.

"Then what's that hanging from a chain about your neck? A bell, it's plain," retorted the Poet rather impatiently.

Alice looked and saw that there *was* a tiny bell, about the size of a thimble, hanging from a very fine chain about her neck, though how it got there she couldn't possibly imagine. "If that's a fire-bell it must be a *very* young one," she said, smiling, and her satisfaction at having made this amusing conjecture quite restored her usual good humour. Curious to see what sort of a tinkle such a diminutive bell would make, Alice gently shook the chain. Instantly a deafening, crashing clangour filled the air, frightening the poor child nearly out of her senses. She hastily dropped the little bell, and, after one last tremendous, echoing peal, the ringing stopped.

The Poet, who seemed to be shaking under his disguise with suppressed laughter, now remarked very gravely: "Well, *what* a voice for one so *young*; I thought at first 'Big Ben' had rung!" And, after a moment's pause, he added: "The Fireman should soon be here to rescue you—but *look*, my dear; a snow storm's starting. Really though it looks to me like *paper* snow!"

And sure enough, the air was soon full of little curled-up strips of paper such as come inside of "snapper mottoes".

"Oh," cried Alice excitedly, "I do hope they have proverbs on them, it will be *such* fun!" She picked up several of the paper snowflakes and, straightening one out, found the following rather disappointing line printed in small red letters:

THE PENGUIN IS MIGHTIER THAN THE SWORD-FISH.

She handed it to the Poet, saying doubtfully, "Perhaps *this* one was meant especially for you;" then half to herself, "it sounds familiar, but that isn't quite the usual wording, I'm sure."

The Poet took the slip and after reading it aloud several times very thoughtfully and slowly, he said with great complacency: "A very proper proverb that, and *how* 'twill irritate Old Spratt—he takes the Sword-fish part, you see—

you're Aunt Crusader—as for me—perhaps you know, my dear, that *I'm* the Hero in the Pantomime."

Alice recollected that the Candlestick-maker had said something about being late to a rehearsal of some sort and she wondered if it were this Pantomime that he had referred to. She was too much interested in the snowflake mottoes, however, to ask about it just then. Unrolling another of the slips, she read aloud:

HONEY MAKES THE HAIR GROW.

"Of course, *that's* just nonsense," she said impatiently; "though, come to think, I *have* heard a proverb something like it—'Money makes the mare go', I believe it was."

"Well," said her companion judicially, "perhaps that other, too, is true, although the wording's tricky; for honey *in the comb*, you know, would make the hair grow—sticky!"

"Perhaps you can tell what *this* one means, too," said Alice, smiling, at the ingenious explanation of the other:

DON'T COUNT YOUR CHICKENS BEFORE YOU PUT ALL
YOUR EGGS IN ONE BASKET

After a moment's reflection, the Poet replied: "In counting chickens, don't you see, there's apt to be some slip—that is, if on arithmetic you've not the firmest grip. And if you *slip* why, like as not, upon your eggs you fall, and if those eggs are in one lot, it's plain you'll break them all!"

Alice was growing very much interested in this game of explanations. "It's my turn," she now exclaimed, "and here's one that I can almost understand myself; it says,

IT'S NEVER TOO STRAIGHT TO BEND

and I daresay *that* means—" She was interrupted by the sudden appearance of a head and shoulders above the edge of the parapet and the next moment a stocky fellow, unmistakably a fireman, stepped from the ladder and stood before them, panting. His shirt was the brightest crimson Alice had ever seen and he wore a big tin fire-hat, the brim of which extended like a wide shovel at the back. Hanging from his belt were a small pick-axe, a brass fire-trumpet, and a leather bucket about half full of water.

"Two of 'em to save," the Fireman muttered complainingly when he had recovered his breath, "*TWO* of 'em—and me on a holiday!" Then taking the bucket from his belt in a business-like way, he dashed the water over the Poet, saying mournfully as he did so, "and not even enough water for *one*."

"I'm glad of that," thought Alice, "though the Poet doesn't seem to much mind being soaked."

The Poet, who apparently had hardly noticed the unexpected bath, was saying cheerfully,

"Don't bother about *me*; I'll flap down to the ground. Help her, old chap."

Then, holding up the bottomless bird cage, he went on, "My helmet for the Pantomime; so glad I thought of it in time."

"He certainly didn't have that cage a moment ago," thought Alice confusedly. "I didn't know that old thing was yours," she started to say, but the Poet, in his awkward penguin disguise, had hopped to the parapet, and now, after a few preliminary flappings of his unwieldy wings, flew heavily away. He had left the bird cage behind and the Fireman, picking it up, hurled it after him with a loud shout of "Heads below!" Then turning to Alice, who half feared that she was about to be thrown after the cage, he said politely enough, but in a rather bored voice, which plainly showed that he did not enjoy working like this while on a holiday, "Well, Miss, what'll it be for *you*, ladder or life net?"

Now Alice did not like the idea of either method of descent, but she felt at least she was *somewhat* familiar with ladders while she had never even seen a life net. "And that ladder," she reasoned, "must lead to *some*where, after all, for the Fireman came up that way." So she finally answered rather doubtfully, "I think I prefer the ladder, if you don't mind."

"Did you say the *ladder* or the *latter*, Miss?" inquired the Fireman, who had been busy readjusting the things on his belt. "Though come to think," he added, "It doesn't really make much difference, *as there ain't any life net*, Miss."

He jammed his hat down, gave a last twitch to his belt and exclaimed, with more animation than Alice had seen him exhibit, "Well, Miss, ladder it is then!" And the next moment Alice found to her surprise that she was enjoying the very agreeable sensation of sliding, at a pleasurable speed, down a smooth, straight bannister. In a strangely silent mist all about her, the paper snow was still falling....

CHAPTER XI

The Skating Party

fter sliding for what seemed miles and miles, Alice was just about to begin a conversation with herself to relieve the lonesome stillness, when she was quite startled to hear a familiar voice nearby exclaim: "I trust we're getting near the ground—these wings work poorly, I have found."

Looking up over her shoulder, Alice saw the Poet floundering along through the air. He seemed to be having some difficulty in steering himself, but, on the whole, was doing remarkably well considering his short flipper-like wings, though his flying did perhaps look more like a sort of slow aerial tumble. A little above him was the bird cage, drifting down through the air as lightly as though it had been made of paper.

"Ca'n't you get hold of the bannister?" called Alice as he flopped nearer. "It would be much easier for you to slide I'm sure."

The Poet, as if seriously considering this suggestion, scratched his head thoughtfully with his wing. This, of course, caused him to fall through the air in an alarmingly lopsided way for quite a distance. When he had steadied himself somewhat again, he shouted: "I'm really afraid that it's too long a jump from here, and besides, at the bottom you—" BUMP!!

The bannister coming to an abrupt end, Alice had landed in a surprisingly painless manner on a surface of very smooth ice, where, owing to the momentum gained in her long descent, she slid backward, in a sitting position, at great speed.... As she started to slow down—after going for what seemed a tremendous distance—Alice heard a confused sound of cheering, and hoarse shouts of "Bravo!" "Wonderful!" and "Very well done, Miss!" growing nearer and nearer. And looking up, as she finally came to a stop, found herself in the midst of an excited group of curiously-dressed animals and people, some of whom she had already met on her strange adventures and others whom she recognized only because she had seen their pictures in her *Mother Goose*.

Most of the group had on skates of a very antiquated pattern, curled up in a large spiral at the toe. The manner of wearing these was in some cases decidedly unusual! Alice noticed particularly a Clown who wore his skates on his *hands*, and the "Old-Man-all-dressed-in-Leather" (Alice felt sure it was he, at any rate), a wrinkled old fellow with only *one* skate, but that an enormous one, strapped to a great shoe which he wore in place of a coat. This necessitated a very strange method of skating—as the illustration shows.

The Old-Man-all-dressed-in-Leather propelled himself forward as Alice rose to her feet after her long slide; he pinned to the quilt, which was still wrapped about her, a large, blue rosette from which hung a long end of ribbon bearing the word WINNER, exclaiming with a good deal of flourish, as he did so: "We compliment you, ma'am, on your most commendable performance and well-earned victory!"

The cheering, which had been hushed during the Old Man's little presentation speech, now broke out afresh and Alice, who had stood grinning sheepishly while the Old Man pinned on the rosette, could not help finally laughing outright at the absurdity of the whole situation; for, to cap the climax, the Poet, in his clumsy penguin disguise, had appeared hopping heavily toward them, rolling the rickety, clattering bird cage ahead of him across the ice.

As Alice stood watching his approach and laughing uncontrollably, a voice, which she recognized as Captain Tee Wee's, boomed out, "All entries for the second race this way!" No one seemed to pay the slightest attention, however, either to this announcement or to the approaching penguin, for the Fireman, whom Alice now noticed for the first time, had started a bonfire on the ice, a short distance away, and the crowd was hastening in that direction. A little bent old woman with an old fashioned "witch-broom" was industriously sweeping up the paper snowflakes that had fallen on the ice (it was a pile of these that the Fireman had lighted).

When Alice approached he stopped his work of tending fire and said in a rather apologetic way, as though he felt that he had been caught at a very childish pastime, "It's a real change, as you can easy understand, Miss, this *lighting* fires—me being on a holiday—for other times I'm mostly busy a-puttin' of 'em out; besides which I've arranged this here fire so's the smoke's all a-blowin' his way, in hopes to wake him up."

Here the Fireman pointed to a little wooden bench nearby. Upon this bench Alice was somehow not at all surprised to see the Milkman stretched out, still snoring loudly.

"We've done about everything else, Miss," went on the Fireman in a discouraged voice, "but it's amazin' how sound-like milkmen does sleep in the daytime."

While the Fireman was speaking, Alice had observed a large red cow—evidently a new arrival—skating toward them in a leisurely way. She was a raw-boned, powerful animal, with skates on all four of her feet and even an extra one fastened on near the end of her frowsy tail! ("I ca'n't see what use *that* one is to her," thought Alice.) Apparently unconscious of the fact that she skated in an awkward, sprawling manner, the cow wore an air of haughty superiority.

Just as Alice was about to call the Fireman's attention to this ridiculous creature, she felt a nudge, and turning, saw that the Captain and the Cook had joined them.

"Souse my tarry pigtail if there ain't old Moolygeezer, the Milkman's crazy cow!" exclaimed the Captain in what he perhaps *intended* for a whispering voice.

"An' prouder-like than ever since the Poet wrote them verses about her jumpin' over the moon," put in the Cook, who seemed to be having a difficult time adjusting his skates, which were, as a matter of fact, not really skates, but long soup ladles.

Moolygeezer, who was now laboriously attempting a figure-eight, evidently overheard the Captain's uncomplimentary stage whisper, for she tossed her head contemptuously. In so doing she lost her precarious balance and fell to the ice with a crash, her cowbell, which heretofore had only tinkled, now jangling loudly as she went down directly in front of the bench on which lay her sleeping master. Roused by the sound of the cowbell the Milkman sat up jerkily, and after looking wildly about in a sleep-dazed way for a moment or two, he spied the cow who was just getting angrily to her feet again amid general laughter and jeering. With a hoarse cry of "I've got you now, you old moon-jumper!" the Milkman made a desperate lunge for the cow's tail, but missed it, falling on the ice.

Though evidently greatly hampered by her skates, Moolygeezer started off with a series of great galloping leaps, and the most ridiculous chase that Alice had ever taken part in began.

By the time the crowd of strangely assorted skaters had gotten their wits together sufficiently to start after her, the ungainly creature was crashing along over the ice at an amazing rate of speed, now running on all fours, and now coasting, as it were, on her hind legs, using her tail when she did this as a sort of rudder.

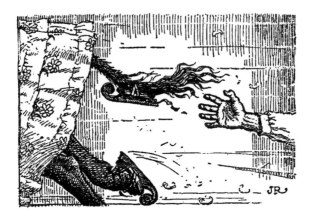

Most of the pursuers, in their frenzied efforts to get started quickly, had fallen down like the Milkman, whom Alice heard muttering wistfully, as he picked himself up and started after the others, "It's werry disappointing, werry."

Not wishing to be left alone, and quite interested, besides, to see how the chase would end, Alice ran along after the noisy crowd.

The Old-Man-dressed-all-in-Leather, notwithstanding his curiously attached single skate, led the pursuit by a good distance. ("Perhaps it's because, skating on his back in the way he does, he ca'n't very well fall down," said Alice to herself.) Next came the Clown, who was going along very smoothly and gracefully on his hands, fanning himself industriously all the while with a large palm-leaf fan which he held somehow with one of his feet. Behind him came the Captain, fairly bellowing with delirious enjoyment of the chase; then the Cook on his soup-ladle skates, and the Poet (he was now *wearing* his bird-cage helmet instead of rolling it) clumsily hopping and flying by turns. Close behind the Poet came the Fireman, shouting a confusion of orders through his brass trumpet.

Strung along after this leading group were many others, some of whom Alice did not remember having seen on the ice before, but who all looked vaguely familiar; one of these last was a round-faced little man carrying a hammer and saw and a number of other tools. He seemed to be skating with the greatest difficulty and was going very slowly. Alice was not surprised at this when she saw that his skates were made entirely of wood. She also saw a large black "'J" painted on the back of his coat, and, remembering the line "J was a joiner", decided that this must be he.

The poor fellow finally stopped, removed his wooden skates and was examining them in a disappointed way when Alice caught up. (She was now very much out of breath and had slowed down to a fast walk.)

Upon seeing her, the Joiner politely raised his little square topped white hat, saying in a very gentlemanly way as he fell into step, "May I be permitted to join this little party?

"You see, *joining* is my trade," he added, as if to explain any seeming boldness in making his request.

"Of course you may; but I'm quite alone," replied Alice, rather puzzled by his reference to the "little party", "or, at least, I *was* alone a second ago," she added doubtfully, looking behind her as though half expecting to see several hitherto unnoticed companions.

"Why, I should call *you* rather a *little* party," explained the Joiner. "That is," he went on hastily, as though fearing that Alice might not have liked this way of putting it, "you're not so *very* large, you know."

"Oh, I see, it was a sort of joke," said Alice, smiling.

"Well," answered her companion thoughtfully, "perhaps it was. But *these* are no joke at any rate." He held up the wooden skates which he was now carrying in his hand.

"They *didn't* seem to slide along very easily," said Alice, feeling that some sympathetic remark was expected of her.

"And I spent days and days selecting the very slipperiest kind of slippery-elm to make them of," said the other with a regretful sigh. "Have some, do," he added sadly, handing one of the skates to Alice and starting to chew on the other in an absent sort of way.

As the Joiner ceased speaking, Alice's ears caught a sound quite different from that of the noisy pursuit, which was now almost out of earshot. It was the ominous soughing of an approaching wind storm which seemed to be coming up behind them. She looked over her shoulder and was really terrified at the threatening look of an oncoming bank of darkness which seemed about to overtake and envelop them.

"Oh, dear! *Whatever* shall we do?" cried the poor child piteously, turning to the Joiner. He was gone!

Alice had no time to soliloquize on his sudden disappearance, for the fast rising wind soon began to blow her along at constantly increasing speed, and, when she glanced once more behind her, the bank of darkness had taken on much the look of an onrushing crowd of screaming, black giants, and moreover, great cracks were appearing in the ice on all sides.

"If only there was *something* to hold on to," groaned Alice who was now fairly flying along. And as if in cruel answer to her wish, there suddenly appeared, sticking up out of one of the cracks just ahead of her a pole bearing a signboard lettered, DANGER! In a moment she would be upon it! As Alice stretched out her hands to ward off the pole, the ice which had been getting very wobbly gave way beneath her with a curious, tinkling crash like the breaking of thin glass—and all was darkness....

Ice gave way beneath her with a curious tinkling crash.

The next thing she knew, the astonished child found herself sitting up unhurt on the damp floor of a large greenhouse.

CHAPTER XII

Strange Growths
and a Stupid Snail

*L*ooking up, Alice saw that there was a jagged hole in the high glass roof above her head. "That's where I came through, I suppose," she began saying to herself as she started to get to her feet, "though I don't see how I—" Here she was interrupted by the unpleasant sensation of a hot, thick fluid splattering down her arm, and turning to discover from whence this came, Alice saw that just behind her was a tall, sturdy bush covered with the largest and strangest blue and white blossoms.

"They look just like big bowls," she thought; then after examining one more closely, added aloud: "Why, they *are* bowls; but what's more, they're all full of gruel!"

The gruel bush was really a very pretty sight, for every one of the big blue and white bowls was full of appetizing yellow gruel, the steam from which was rising in beautiful delicate rings and spirals (as the branches were now trembling a little).

"I probably jarred it when I came through the roof," said Alice sagely, "and it was some of the hot gruel that splattered on my arm. Now this," she went on to herself in an amusingly chatty way, "is what I call a very *practical* bush." Reaching up, she carefully picked one of the bowl blossoms, taking care to break off quite a length of stem to hold it by. When  Alice did this she noticed that the bowl was conveniently provided with a silver spoon, which stood up in the middle of the thick fluid contents like the pistil of a flower.

As the appetizing odor of the steaming gruel had made her extremely hungry, Alice, of course, wished to sample it at once. She found, however, that it was far too hot to be eaten.

"I can look about the greenhouse while I wait for it to cool off a bit," she told herself; "for there may be other flowers here just as interesting and practical as these."

Near the gruel bush was a curious growth which proved to be a clay-pipe plant. This did not interest the little girl particularly, but observing that these pipes were exactly the same as the one the Snipe had lost, she picked one, thinking that, if she met him again, he might like to have it to replace the other.

Next to the clay-pipe plant, and near the door of the greenhouse, grew a vine upon which hung what looked, at first glance, to be only rather large gourds; but as Alice came nearer she saw to her surprise that they were really quaint little old fashioned fiddles. Just as she was about to pick one of these to add to her unusual bouquet, she heard, not far off, sounds as though someone were pounding insistently upon a door and now and then angrily demanding admission in a loud voice.

She carefully picked one of the bowl blossoms.

As the sounds came from somewhere outside the greenhouse, Alice, without waiting to pick one of the fiddles, opened the nearby door and stepped out.

She now found herself on a narrow grass-grown path bordered by neat little signs about a foot high, set close together. All of these signs bore the same words:

"Keep *On* The Grass."

On each side of the grassy walk was a sort of shallow moat almost full of dirty, slimy water, and beyond this, in place of trees, were rows of large, open green umbrellas, standing upright.

The path led directly to the ornate front door of a smallish but showy sort of palace, at no great distance, and in front of this door stood Doctor Foster. (Alice recognized him at once, for he was exactly like his picture.) He seemed to be in a great state of impatience and was pounding vigorously on the door with the handle of his umbrella, which was bright green like those standing beyond the moat.

Alice, who had by this time come to within a few rods of the palace, was about to call out to the Doctor, when without any

warning the path she was on started, with sudden violence, to swing from side to side—like a hammock that has been given an unexpected jerk—and almost before she realized what was happening the poor child found herself sliding off into the slimy water, which luckily was only up to her knees at this point.

The path stopped swaying almost immediately and Alice scrambled back onto it and ran the remaining distance to the castle door, feeling somehow very angry and foolish at the same time.

The Doctor, who, in spite of his pounding and shouting, had heard the commotion of Alice's mishap, had dropped his umbrella and was already opening his little black medicine satchel when she arrived, panting. (She was much surprised to find that she still held the pipe and bowl; the contents of the bowl had changed mysteriously to what looked like cider in which a small crab was swimming about.)

"Just what happened to me a few minutes ago—just what happened to me, and a poor sort of joke, too, *I* say," the Doctor remarked without looking up. "Now where *did* I—ah, *here* it is!" he added, taking from his satchel a small blue bottle labelled, "FOR WET FEET". And before Alice had time to protest he clapped it to her lips and emptied the entire contents down her throat. Then putting the empty bottle back in his satchel he turned again to the door, only pausing for a moment to say very seriously, "You know, my child, there's *nothing* so dangerous as wet feet—nothing so dangerous. Why, I once knew a centipede—" But here he resumed his battering at the door panels and the rest of the centipede story was drowned out by the din.

The medicine had apparently started to do its work immediately, for already Alice felt a very decided sensation of warmth in her feet, and a thick cloud of steam had begun to rise from them. This steaming continued violently for about half a minute, and when it stopped she found that her shoes and stockings were perfectly dry.

By this time the Doctor had broken his umbrella and was sitting in a discouraged way on the doorstep, absently swallowing, two or three at a time, some large red capsules from a box labelled "PARR'S PATIENCE PILLS—Take one every 24 hours."

Alice was about to remind him that he was taking what seemed to her entirely too many of these, when the door opened inward and the Doctor, who had been resting his back against it, fell back sprawling, colliding as he did so with an

enormous snail—about four feet tall—which wore, in addition to the usual shell, a rather jaunty little red hat, with DOORMAN lettered upon it.

Through the open door Alice, to her astonishment looked, not into a dark hallway or a room, as she had expected to, but into what seemed to be a kind of formal garden, at the far end of which, behind a hedge of huge sunshades, she could now hear the sound of many voices. The castle, in fact, consisted of only one wall and was not much more substantial than a piece of scenery.

The strange doorman, with scarcely a glance at Alice or the sprawling Doctor, very deliberately picked up three or four of the pills, which had scattered in all directions, and began munching them with a sort of dreamy satisfaction.

The Doctor, who had risen to his feet, waited with great patience until the Snail had entirely satisfied his appetite for the pills and then said very meekly: "You will pardon my knocking, I feel sure—you see, I have an appointment with the King; but really you needn't have *hurried* so, my man."

The surprised Alice wondered whether the Doctor's suddenly acquired docility of manner was due to the great number of PARR'S PATIENCE PILLS he had eaten or to the rather threatening appearance of the Snail's long horns.

Without giving any evidence that he had even heard the Doctor's humble remarks, the Snail laboriously took from the lining of his hat a small, fat, leather-covered book entitled, "DOOR RULES, VOL. VII," and began thumbing over the pages. While he was doing this, Alice noticed that on the wall near the door hung a placard which read, "COURT JESTERS WANTED: APPLY BETWEEN 12 and 12, K. C."

At the end of a full minute the Snail cleared his throat and, with an air of solemn importance, read: "RULE 149. No one is allowed to pass in unless he leaves his umbrella at the door." He then languidly motioned to the Doctor to drop his umbrella and enter, and drew back very deliberately to allow him to pass; but when Alice started to follow, the Snail, to her surprise, refused to let her pass.

"Orders is orders, Miss," he said in a stupid voice, and then recited very slowly the rule he had just read.

"But *I haven't* any umbrella," exclaimed Alice, much annoyed at all this delay. ("Though as I don't know *where* I'm going," she told herself, "I don't suppose there's really any great hurry about getting there!")

"Then you'll have to go back and get one, Miss," said the Snail stubbornly, repeating for the third time, "No one is allowed to pass in unless he leaves his umbrella at the door. And even if she had one to leave," he added reflectively, speaking aloud, but to himself, "it wouldn't be *his* umbrella, it would be *her* umbrella."

This, to the Snail's way of thinking, seemed to settle the matter, for he turned without another word and started to close the door. He did this so slowly, however, that Alice had time to reflect—"I can slip by him while his back is turned, and, being a snail, he'll never be able to catch me." Suiting the action to the thought, she dodged noiselessly past him and ran....

CHAPTER **XIII**

King Cole's Court

*A*lice raced down the little path, pausing to look neither to right nor left, until she came to an opening in the hedge of giant sunshades. Here she stopped short, for a curiously picturesque, lively scene, brilliant in colour, met her eyes.

Before her lay a vivid green tennis lawn upon which quite a number of gaily-dressed Mother Goose people and animals, each carrying a Japanese fan and an orange, were moving about with a great deal of merry chatter. Some of the party Alice had seen before, but many were entirely new to her. Among the latter was a gigantic woman, at least ten feet tall, with hands which were immense, even for one of her size. She wore a crinoline-skirted dress of brilliant yellow.

"That must be the Candlestick-maker's wife, Pansy," Alice began saying to herself, "and that pig with wings in the funny old bonnet is—" Her observations were at this point interrupted, however, by a great booming voice calling out, *"PLAY!"*

Then began what proved to be a most confusing and noisy game of tennis.

In the first place almost everyone present—and there were a score or more—took part. The only ones not actually playing were some dwarfish, woodeny soldiers, about three feet in height, all armed with bellows, who stood in a row across the court in place of a net; and four or five court attendants (cats) who busied themselves by continually shifting the white ribbon boundary lines of the tennis court about during the game!

In place of balls and racquets the strange players used the oranges and fans they had been carrying, and their frenzied beating about with the large fans raised a breeze which soon grew to be quite a gale.

Sitting on a very gaudy throne near the far side of the court, Alice had noticed an enormously fat, jolly looking man, dressed in bright scarlet, with a crown on his head and a scepter in his hand—*King Cole*, without a doubt!

The King acted as umpire at first, bawling out rules, decisions and scores, in a voice choking with merriment; but as the ridiculous game proceeded he became more and more hilariously excited and finally leaped from his throne and joined the boisterous contestants, using his scepter as a racquet.

The game now became more confused and noisy than ever, for King Cole, in spite of his great girth, proved to be as lively as a cricket. He bounced about here, there and everywhere, whacking at the flying oranges with loud whoops of joy, and turning a handspring now and then out of pure exuberance.

His contagious enthusiasm caused the others to redouble their exertions and they tore about the court, tripping over the moving boundary tapes and shouting with laughter at the clumsy efforts of some of their number to imitate the acrobatic agility of the King. The ludicrous attempts of one extremely "bandy-legged" man to turn a "cartwheel" caused Alice to almost go into hysterics.

Though most of the fans were broken by this time, neither side seemed to have the advantage. The players had begun throwing the oranges about at each other, and this kept Alice constantly dodging, as she was now standing very near the court in order to watch the game better.

When the uproarious excitement was at its height, King Cole, who had just had his crown knocked awry by a collision with the giantess Pansy, suddenly held up his hand to command order and silence and, when he could get his breath, shouted, in a voice that might easily have been heard a mile away, "REFRESHMENTS!"

At this there was a loud outburst of cheering and hand-clapping and cries of "Long Live King Cole!" in every key. After which most of the tennis players started immediately and noisily to suck the oranges with which they had been playing.

King Cole now turned and started to walk back to the throne, shouting over his shoulder as he went, "We declare the game a tie!" and adding in an aside to a large grey goose who was standing near him, "Our games are *always* ties—everybody happy then, and no unpleasantness."

"I suppose," thought Alice, "now that the game is over the King will notice me, and perhaps I'll be put out." It had suddenly occurred to her that she had not been invited to this tennis party, and furthermore that the Snail Doorman, despite his slowness, might be expected back almost any time now with a report of her breaking of the umbrella rule. She felt rather relieved, therefore, when King Cole, catching sight of her standing near the throne, showed no surprise, but smiled beamingly upon her and beckoned for her to approach.

"Just what we needed, my dear, *just* what we needed!" he exclaimed, joyfully rubbing his hands together; and taking the bowl and pipe which Alice had almost forgotten she was holding—he settled himself upon the throne with a deep sigh of happiness; then, motioning Alice to a place near him on the edge of the little circular dais upon which the throne stood, King Cole cried jovially, "*Everybody* be seated!"

Alice saw with surprise that the Soldiers alone disregarded this royal command and remained standing stolidly in line as before, and she felt that here was a good opportunity to begin a conversation—a friendly chat with a *King* would be something she could boast about a little, afterward—so she asked in her very politest manner: "Please, Your Majesty, why don't the Soldiers sit down like the rest?"

The King had broken off a long piece of the pipe stem and through this he was contentedly sucking up the contents of the bowl.

Upon hearing Alice's question, he removed the pipe stem from his lips to say with a chuckle, "Oh, it's all right about *them*, my dear. You see, that's our standing army and naturally, a *standing* army *ca'n't* sit down."

Most of the guests must have been familiar with this little joke of King Cole's, for many of them had started to laugh extravagantly as soon as Alice asked her question. This seemed to encourage the King, who waited until the applause had ceased and then continued complacently: "We suppose you've noticed, my dear, that our Soldiers are all armed with bellows? (A rather clever idea of our own, that.) Perhaps you can guess the reason, eh?" Then, without waiting more than a second or two for an answer from poor Alice—who was beginning to feel uncomfortably conspicuous and extremely stupid—the King said triumphantly: "It's so that without the expense of ammunition they can always return blow for blow."

At this, the Soldiers all suddenly raised their pairs of bellows and squeezed them in perfect unison, with a most surprising result! All of the party sitting in front of the "army" on the tennis lawn, with the exception of the ponderous Pansy, were rolled over and over by the blast, and there was a great deal of squealing and laughter and good natured scrambling about to recover lost hats and oranges.

King Cole fairly rocked with his enjoyment of this lively scene.

In the midst of all this uproar, Alice noticed coming through a nearby opening in the sunshade hedge, a roly-poly little old lady wearing a crown like the King's and a very soiled robe of light lavender velvet, trimmed with ermine. Behind her walked the cook of the *Summersault Sally*, carrying a plate piled high with slices of bread, and a tremendous jar labelled "HONEY". They had almost reached the throne by the time the King, who had caught sight of them when they first appeared, managed to control his mirth and shout to the boisterous guests on the lawn, "Silence—the Queen!

"Of course, we don't mean by that that she needs *silencing*, you understand," he whispered loudly, turning to Alice with a jolly wink; "that is, not just *now*, perhaps—though she *is* something of a talker, my dear."

The Queen, who had evidently overheard this last remark,

seemed to take it as a great compliment. She hastily swallowed all she possibly could of a large bite she had just taken from a slice of bread and honey—which the cook had handed to her a moment before—and said coyly, with her mouth still half full: "You see, my child, he's a great Hatterer. Oh yes, indeed, a most atrocious flatterer; but there *is* truth in what he just said about my being a wonderful talker—Not so stingy with that honey, my good fellow" (this to the Cook.) "Why, once in my younger days, I remember talking from seven in the morning until ten in the evening to an admirer of mine—deaf he was—and never even—" Here the Queen took another prodigious bite of bread and honey, and though she kept right on talking, her mouth was so full that for a time one could only catch an almost unintelligible word now and then.

Alice soon gathered from gestures, however, that the Queen had changed the subject, and was now expressing extravagant admiration for the ridiculous, ragged old quilt which Alice still wore.

"I really don't need the quilt any longer, now that it has grown so much warmer," thought Alice, "and besides, her Majesty really *does* need a large napkin of some sort." So she removed the gaudy covering, and was quite surprised to hear herself saying, "I beg of you to accept this trifling gift, for what your Majesty admires is yours."

She vaguely remembered having read these words somewhere, but they seemed to fit the situation perfectly.

The Queen seemed quite overcome with astonished gratitude, for her jaws even stopped working and she stared at the quilt as though doubtful whether the offer of so rich a gift were meant seriously. Then suddenly—regardless of the bread and honey, with which both her hands and her mouth were now full—she threw her short arms about Alice and kissed her heartily on both cheeks!

"That's a great honour for you, my dear child, a great honour!" chuckled the King; then with another of his elaborate winks, added: "I suppose you'll be very much stuck up for a while." Then finishing his refreshment with a loud smacking of lips and a tremendous sigh of satisfaction, the rotund Monarch hurled the empty bowl over the hedge, and then placing his fore-fingers against his teeth he whistled ear-split tingly. ("Just the way our baker's boy does it," thought Alice.)

The King's whistle was apparently a signal, for immediately the cat-attendants appeared at the entrance to the court, dragging a small wheeled platform upon which stood a huge, gaily-painted band-box at least six feet in diameter. The attendants stopped in front of the throne and the crowd of guests threw away their oranges and formed an expectant 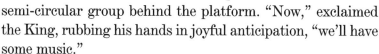 semi-circular group behind the platform. "Now," exclaimed the King, rubbing his hands in joyful anticipation, "we'll have some music."

"His Majesty *dotes* on good music," the Queen remarked to Alice, "though it usually puts him to sleep—that is, when the band plays loud enough, and this one always does—except—"

"But where are the musicians?" Alice interrupted, puzzled; "I'm sure I don't see any band."

"Why, the *band's* in the *band-box*, silly," chuckled King Cole, who had overheard her query, "where a band *should* be. Now, if you'll listen—"

Just then there was a sort of "musical explosion", as Alice expressed it afterward, and the cover of the band-box flew off and went skimming over the hedge. Standing in the box, with only their heads and shoulders visible, were the famous "Fiddlers Three" and the Piper and his son Tom; and seated on the Piper's shoulder was none other than Alice's old friend, the Candlestick-maker, with his drum.

Each one of these zealous musicians seemed to be trying desperately to drown out the other five, and the Candlestick-maker, having the noisiest instrument, was almost succeeding in doing this.

Alice soon recognized the tune (though they were playing it at about twice its usual speed) as *"Over the Hills and Far Away"*. In response to the enthusiastic applause of the audience, the band kept repeating this one air over and over in a very monotonous fashion, the only variation being that at each repetition they went a little faster.

"I suppose," thought Alice, "the reason is that it's the only tune the Piper's son can play, and probably King Cole doesn't mind anyhow as long as they make plenty of noise. Why, he's nodding already," she added. "I'm sure I *never* saw so many sleepy heads as there are in this country."

And sure enough, as the Queen had predicted, the King, after a minute or two of the noisy "music" was sleeping quite peacefully. Upon the crowd of guests, however, it had a very different effect, for they all began a very lively and curious kind of square dance, the principal figure in which was like a combination of the games of Ring-around-a-Rosy and Snap-the-Whip.

Just then there was a sort of musical explosion.

When the band, apparently exhausted by its efforts, finally stopped playing, the Queen—who was always either eating or talking—hastily gulped down the last of the supply of bread and honey and turned to Alice. "While the musicians are resting between selections," she said, pleasantly, "we *usually* play games; and as you, my dear (here she unexpectedly kissed the poor child again heartily), are the guest of honour today, we shall leave the choice of the first game to you; although," she rattled on, "*I* should strongly suggest 'Stage Coach'. That's a *delightful* game, my dear, and a great favourite of mine. Such a lot of *talking* in it, too, you know."

"If you'd just as soon," ventured Alice, "I'd like to start—" She was about to say that she would like to start with a game of "Blindman's Buff". "Just imagine what fun it would be played by *this* crowd," she had thought. The talkative Queen, however, did not wait for the little girl to finish the sentence, but exclaimed enthusiastically: "You'd like to start right now, of course, my dear. Well, so we can and so we shall." Then, motioning the crowd to be seated on a number of little blue three-legged stools, which the attendants had just brought in and placed near the throne, she announced: "This young lady has especially requested that we now play 'Stage Coach', which happens to be a game of which I, too, am particularly fond."

As some of the younger readers of this tale may never have played the amusing old-fashioned game of "Stage Coach", let me explain it in a few words.

Before the game begins the "parts" are given out: that is, each player is given the name of one of the characters in a story of an adventurous stage coach trip. Excepting the *leader*—the one who recites or reads the "story"—the players are all seated. Whenever during the recitation of the adventures any one of the characters is mentioned, the player having that "part" rises from his seat, turns around twice and sits down again, the failure to do this calling for a forfeit. Whenever the word "*Stage Coach*" is heard, *all* rise and change seats, the "leader" trying in the general scramble to obtain a seat for himself. If the leader succeeds in this, the player left standing must go on with the story.

Alice took a seat among the others on one of the little stools and the Queen gave out the "parts," her haphazard distribution of these causing a great deal of merriment. To the gigantic Pansy, for example, she gave the part of the "Little Dog" (a traditional "Stage Coach" character) and to Jack Spratt that of ponderous "Captain Swordfish"; while Alice herself was old "Aunty Crusader", and many of the others had parts equally inappropriate.

When all were ready, the Queen started to read very rapidly from a book which she had taken from a pocket in her skirt, and the game began.

Alice happened to be sitting between the tremendous Pansy and the Old Man of Bombay. This proved to be rather an unfortunate thing for her, as the Old Man, growing very much excited as the game progressed, puffed harder and harder on his pipe, filling the air with such a dense cloud of curling smoke that the little girl could only now and then catch a glimpse of the Queen and the other players. The giantess occupied not only her own stool but about two thirds of Alice's, most of the time, and this kept the child

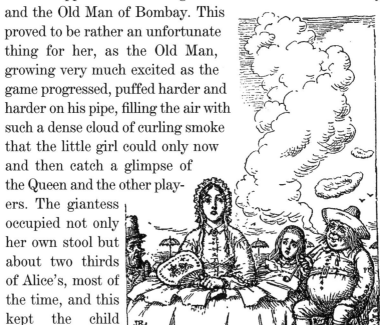

terribly worried; for in the course of the story the "Little Dog" was mentioned more often any of the other characters, and Pansy was therefore continually having to get up, turn, and sit down again. "And it's almost *certain* that sooner or later she'll sit down right on top of poor little me," said Alice to herself; "and if she ever does—" But just then the story reached the point where Captain Swordfish said, "Where is the big cheese we brought along for our lunch?" "I'm afraid," answered the Footman, "that the Little Dog has eaten it, sir!" The giantess, who was doubtless growing rather angry at having to get up so much oftener than the others, reseated herself this time with a petulant flounce and the little stool gave way beneath her weight! At the same instant, as if to make the occurrence more dramatic, the music began again with a long, rolling rub-a-dub-a-dub-dub from the drum, and the Old Man of Bombay blew such a blinding cloud of smoke from his pipe that for a few moments Alice could see nothing....

CHAPTER XIV

The Rehearsal of "The Enchanted Cheese"

*T*he smoke had changed to a thick cloud of dust, and when this cleared away somewhat, Alice saw that everything else had changed remarkably, too.

She was now sitting in the midst of a curiously-costumed, jostling crowd on top of a lumbering stage coach. Though the people and animals in this party were the same ones she had just been with at King Cole's Court (except that Pansy had disappeared), Alice observed that their clothes had changed strangely, all having now a swollen, padded outlook which gave, even to the attenuated Jack Spratt, a ridiculously puffy appearance. The little girl herself felt as though her dress were stuffed out with pillows.

From beneath her, inside the coach, Alice could hear the band playing discordantly; fortunately the sound was somewhat muffled.

"I suppose the windows are closed, and I'm *very* thankful for that," she remarked to Doctor Foster, who was sitting next her. "And I'm also thankful that I'm not inside, even though it is so crowded up here."

"It's these puffed-up clothes everybody's wearing that makes it so crowded," replied the Doctor (he was now about the shape of a balloon, himself). "You see, my child, the reason for these full clothes is that this is to be a *full dress* rehearsal; but the stage really ought to be bigger. Why, I once knew a man who got *hemmed* in by a crowd and he's had a *stitch in his side* ever since!"

"Oh, then *this* must be the rehearsal the Candlestick-maker spoke of," began Alice, delighted at the prospect of "theatricals". "And, come to think of it, the Poet said something about—" Here she was interrupted by the Poet himself, who rose in his seat and began to shout: "Friends, fellow citizens: silence, please! We're going to rehearse 'The Enchanted Cheese'." (The Poet was still dressed as a penguin, and his ridiculous bird cage "helmet" was set at a rakish angle on his head.) "Curtain goes up on the opening scene," he went on, "showing a grocery. Enter Queen."

At this juncture the stage coach, which had evidently just then struck a very rough piece of road, began to bounce and bang along so noisily that Alice, who was sitting on the back seat, could catch only a few words now and then of what the Poet was saying. Then, too, the dust became so thick that at times she could scarcely see anything at all, so that afterwards the memory of the "rehearsal" was always confused and unsatisfactory. She gathered, however, from the parts of the first act that she *did* hear and see, that the plot of the pantomime had to do principally with the chase of an

enchanted Stilton cheese, which had escaped from the Queen's buttery. And this seemed to necessitate, on the part of the actors, a great deal of tripping over each other's feet and falling down and throwing things about.

"In the first place," said Alice, in telling her sister about it all afterward, "there was a good deal of quarreling about who should have the parts with the most *eating* in them, and when the 'rehearsing' finally started it was *very* much like the game of 'Stage Coach' we had just been playing at King Cole's Court, for as each different character in the pantomime was mentioned by the Poet, the one taking that part would jump up and go through all sorts of strange antics; and the top of the stage was *so* crowded and we were rocking so from side to side, that quite often some one would be pushed off! Though I don't suppose the fall could have hurt any of them much, as their clothes were all padded out so."

After this sort of thing had been going on for about ten minutes the coach began to slow down, the noise of the band inside diminishing at the same time. Soon both the stage coach and the music stopped.

When the dust had settled, Alice, looking forward, was astonished to see that there were no horses hitched to their strange conveyance.

"It almost seems as though it must have been the music that kept us going," said Alice aloud to herself, "for when the band stopped, the stage stopped."

The Doctor, who was now rummaging about in his little medicine satchel, overheard this remark and said without looking up: "Of course, a stage coach ca'n't go without noise, silly. But *this'll* soon revive that band, I daresay," he added, "and then we can go on again." As he said this, he pulled out of his satchel a small bottle labelled, "EXCELO'S ELIXER FOR EXHAUSTED MUSICIANS." He then climbed down the little steps on the side of the coach, opened the door and stepped in.

Most of the actors had.by this time jumped down to the ground and were peering anxiously in at the windows in a helpless sort of way.

"If *that* medicine works as quickly as the stuff he gave me for wet feet, we ought to be going again very shortly," said Alice to herself, "though I'm not so tremendously anxious to go on with—" Here there was a sudden deafening burst of drumming, fiddling, and piping, and the stage coach started off with such unexpected violence that Alice was jerked backwards out of her seat—

CHAPTER XV

In the Studio and —

————*a* nd found herself floating through the air like a soap-bubble. She struck lightly on the top of the tall hedge bordering the road, bounced once or twice in a really delightful manner, then drifted along and was finally carried by a gentle breeze, in through the open window of a dear little thatched house that stood just beyond the hedge.

Alice landed with scarcely a jolt, on a small table in the middle of a room, which was very evidently an artist's studio; for stacked against the walls were canvases of all sizes, and there were two or three easels standing about. She was just going to jump down to the floor and begin a tour of inspection, when from behind the largest easel stepped a thin, pleasant-faced little gentleman in baggy, paint-daubed corduroy clothes and an extremely long-ended necktie. It was the Artist whom the Snipe had pointed out to her, at the very start of all these adventures, as the maker of the wonderful pictures in *Mother Goose*. ("How *long* ago that *does* seem, too," thought Alice, rather wistfully.) The Artist carried a palette and a curious assortment of brushes: there was a hair-brush, a tooth-brush and a clothes-brush, besides two or three of the sort that house painters generally use. In thinking about this afterward, Alice decided that it was really a very good idea on the part of the Artist. For why *not* use a clothes-brush for painting clothes, a hair-brush for hair, and so on?

"If it's a portrait you're after," said the Artist politely, "I'm afraid you'll have to wait till next week; for as soon as I finish some pictures I'm working on now for the Poet's new book of verses, I've got to start right in on the scenery for that plaguey pantomime. And the worst of *that* is, that the Queen has insisted that, in the grocery scene, all the vegetables must be painted so well that they'll be really *eatable*; and *that's* going to take a lot of time. But, by the way, my child," he added, lowering his voice, "when you came in did you happen to see

anything of an old Wolf hanging around outside the door?"

"Well, sir," answered Alice a little timidly, "I didn't come in through the *door*, but through the window. You see, I fell off the stage coach and—"

"*I* understand," interrupted the Artist, genially; "*you just dropped in*, as one might say. And I see you came down *plump*, too," he added with a smiling glance at the child's strangely balloon-like clothes. "You're a bit puffed up still, I daresay, about having been on the stage. Though you needn't worry about that," he added consolingly, "you'll soon be quite your normal size again, I'm sure."

This seemed indeed to be so, for already her dress had shrunk perceptibly, and Alice was beginning to look more as usual. It still, however, gave her rather a ridiculously blowzy appearance and made her feel uncomfortably self-conscious, especially in the presence of an Artist, so she hastened to change the subject by asking, "Wo'n't you please tell me more about that Wolf you're expecting? Is he a friend of yours?"

"I should say he *isn't* a friend of mine, child," whispered the Artist, glancing apprehensively toward the door. "In fact, he's my *worst* enemy. He's a bill collector, you see, and a most frightful nuisance he is, too, always knocking at the door just when I'm especially anxious not to be disturbed. But speaking of *nuisances*—" (here he chuckled; evidently reminded of something which gave him great satisfaction) "—I *must* tell you about the crows. They used to be a worse nuisance to my neighbour, the Farmer, than that old Wolf is to me; but I've fixed *them*! Yesterday I painted a full length portrait of John O'Gudgeon, the Wildman, and set it up out there in the Farmer's field, as a scarecrow. Those thieving birds wo'n't bother *him* again."

"But I saw some crows flying right by this window just a few seconds ago," put in Alice. "I noticed them particularly, for each one carried a little sack."

"That's just what I was coming to, my child," exclaimed the Artist delightedly. "You see they were so fearfully frightened by that scarecrow of mine that they're even bringing back the grain they stole last summer."

"It must have been a *wonderful* scarecrow," said Alice, laughing.

This complimentary remark evidently pleased the Artist tremendously, for he smiled beamingly and led Alice to the large easel—the one he had been working at before the interruption of her arrival.

Upon the easel was a drawing of a rather timorous young girl dressed in quaint,

JOHN O'GUDGEON

old-fashioned costume and carrying a bucket in her hand. In the background were three or four dogwood trees.

"As I told you before," the Artist remarked affably, "I'm doing the pictures that are to go with the rhymes in the Poet's new book—*More Mother Goose Rhymes*, I think he's going to call it. And this one that I've just finished goes with a verse that starts:—

> *'The murmuring Brook to Betsy said,*
> *"Why have you turned so pale?"*
> *"I thought I heard the dogwood bark,"*
> *Quoth she, "down in the vale."'*

"But you haven't drawn any brook in the picture," ventured Alice, rather timidly.

"Why," exclaimed the Artist, "so I haven't, to be sure; but come to think, it really isn't necessary, for the girl has a pail, you see, so *she* can draw the *water* herself."

"Perhaps," he added, "you'd like to read some of the new rhymes while I'm making the next picture." As he said this, the Artist took from the side pockets of his baggy brown coat several rolled up sheets of the kind of paper Alice remembered writing on with the self-steering pen.

She settled herself comfortably on a soft green rug, smoothed out the sheets and began to read. The following verse is the one that happened to come first:—

NOVELTIES

Pray visit our shop on the side of the hill,
At the sign of the Galloping Door:
Come in and examine and buy if you will
These NOVELTIES, ne'er shown before!
We've muzzles for dogfish and splitters for hairs,
And switches for "beating the Dutch".
We've pills that prevent one from falling downstairs,
And even a clog-dancing crutch.
We keep a contrivance for waking one up
By setting one's pillow afire;
A book of instructions for training a pup
To climb to the top of a spire:
A safety device for exploding ideas,
A guaranteed, smokeless clay pipe,
But better than THAT—a fine, self-raising hat.
And a pattern for cutting up tripe!
Don't fail, please, to notice upon the third shelf,
Right next to the yarn-spinning top,
A wonderful thing I invented myself,
A new SILENT SOUP SPOON! So stop,
Step in for a minute or two and look round,
Our wares we feel sure will surprise,
For we've everything here that is USEFULLY QUEER.
But you've heard of that "WORD TO THE WISE"—

As Alice finished reading, a feeling of homesickness came over her, for she was reminded of the many times she had read

We keep a contrivance for waking one up by setting one's pillow afire.

Mother Goose verses to her pets in the garden at home. "If only I had my dear, dear Pussikins and Patsy here right now," she sighed piteously. Curiously enough, just as she said this, a sudden breeze from the open window disturbed a pile of papers lying on a small stand near which Alice was sitting, and there drifted down to the floor, directly in front of her, a very pretty sketch of two sleeping kittens.

"I can pretend *these* are Pussikins and Patsy," said Alice, trying hard to be cheerful, "and it will be really quite easy, too, for I never saw such a life-like picture."

The Artist, who was tacking a fresh sheet of paper to the drawing board on his easel, overheard this and said, complacently: "It *is* life-like, if I *do* say so. Why, would you believe it, since I drew that picture there hasn't been a mouse in the place, and they used to take my bread and cheese off the shelf, right from under my very nose."

"Perhaps," suggested Alice, smiling at her own idea, "if you'd paint a picture of a large, full grown cat, a real *mouser* like our Thomas, the mice would bring back the bread and cheese just as the crows brought back the corn."

"That's a really *fine* idea, my child," said the Artist, thoughtfully, "and I'll try it just as soon as I get these drawings done."

Alice now set the sketch of the sleeping kittens up against the leg of a nearby stool, and picking up another of the long sheets, she assumed a serious air and said: "Now, children, I want you to be *very* attentive. The *title* of this is, 'An Explanation'." She then very gravely read the following:—

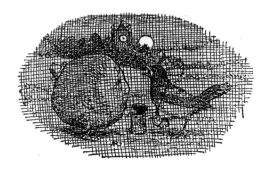

The Early Bird, at two a.m., once met the Rolling Stone:
(I don't exactly envy them their working hours, I own.)
Of course they "passed the time o' day"—or rather, time
  o' night;
Said Stone, "Looks quite like rain, I'd say," and Bird
  replied, "It MIGHT."
They talked of this for quite a while, till confidential
  grown.
The Bird remarked,
  "Look here—don't smile—I'm ENVIOUS, friend Stone.
Folks don't expect a thing of YOU—not even any MOSS,
While, I, 'the worm', howe'er he squirm, must get. It
  makes me cross.
My reputation is at stake. Responsibility I always seem
  to have to take—
  It's slowly killing me."
"I'll gladly occupations change," kind-hearted Stone
  replied;

"To hunt for worms I will arrange."
"And I'll just roll," Bird cried.

*　　　*　　　*　　　*

If you should meet a Rolling Bird, or Early Stone, no
*　　doubt*
'Twould seem absurd, had you not heard just how it
*　　came about.*

When she had finished reading these verses, Alice looked up to see how the Artist's work was progressing, and was astonished to find that he was putting the very last touches on a most spirited illustration.

The picture showed a crowd of Mother Goose characters all dancing gaily about in a large circle.

"There's the Captain," cried Alice, delightedly ,"and the Milkman and the Cow and Doctor Foster—and do *look* at King Cole and the Fiddlers—why, even the Snail's dancing—" Here she stopped short in amazement, for the familiar figures in the drawing had begun to really *move*, slowly at first, but soon faster and faster—and growing larger, too, all the while, as they danced—and finally, led by King Cole and the Fiddlers, the merry, boisterous party leaped, one after another, from the paper on the drawing board down to the floor of the studio, where they formed a ring about Alice and the Artist and continued their capering.

The room now began to expand—the ceiling melted away and changed to blue sky, in which little pink clouds were floating and the walls became more and more like a hedge; even the soft green rug that Alice was sitting on seemed to be turning into a thick-turfed lawn, and the easels into hawthorne trees.

As the dancers circled round and round, the ungainly antics of some of them threw Alice into spasms of uncontrollable laughter. The Milkman's cow, Moolygeezer, was the most irresistibly comic of them all. She was still wearing her skates, and though lurching and tripping ridiculously at almost every step, seemed still to be trying desperately to preserve her haughty, contemptuous manner. Doctor Foster's medicine case had come open and was scattering pills, powders, and bottles in every direction.

The Old-Man-all-dressed-in-Leather was dancing on his back (very much as he had skated). The only one that Alice did not remember having seen before at some stage of her adventures, was a gaunt, hungry-looking Wolf, evidently the dreaded bill collector who had slipped into the studio under cover of the general tumult. The dancers were soon moving so fast that is was impossible to distinguish any individual figures.

"Do *look* at them go! You're missing *such* a sight, my dears," said Alice, turning to the "pretend" kittens. They, too, had come to life, but were still sleeping quietly. (The paper upon which they had been drawn was nowhere to be seen.)

"Wake up, my dears!" cried Alice; and as she said this, she noticed that the sheets of paper in her hand had changed to a book—her own *Mother Goose*!

"Wake up, my dears, wake up!" continued a voice like an echo of her own. She looked up.

The dancers had disappeared; the Artist was putting away his brushes and—but, no—it was not the Artist, it was her own sister, who was saying as she folded up her paintbox, "Wake up, dear. Why, you've been asleep for almost a whole hour."

As the dancers circled round and round…

"*Who'd ever even fancy that so many unusual things could happen in less than an hour?*" said Alice slowly, sitting up and rubbing the sleep out of her eyes.

And that was the end of the story in the book that Betsy found in the attic.

ALSO AVAILABLE FROM EVERTYPE

Alice's Adventures in Wonderland, 2008

Through the Looking-Glass and What Alice Found There
2009

Wonderland Revisited and the Games Alice Played There
by Keith Sheppard, 2009

A New Alice in the Old Wonderland
by Anna Matlack Richards, 2009

Alice's Adventures under Ground, 2009

The Nursery "Alice", 2010

The Hunting of the Snark, 2010

Alice's Adventures in Wonderland,
Retold in words of one Syllable by Mrs J. C. Gorham, 2010

Clara in Blunderland, by Caroline Lewis, 2010

Lost in Blunderland: The further adventures of Clara
by Caroline Lewis, 2010

John Bull's Adventures in the Fiscal Wonderland
by Charles Geake, 2010

The Westminster Alice by H. H. Munro (Saki), 2010

Alice in Blunderland, by John Kendrick Bangs, 2010

Eachtraí Eilíse i dTír na nIontas
Alice in Irish, 2007

Lastall den Scáthán agus a bhFuair Eilís Ann Roimpi
Looking-Glass in Irish, 2009

Alys in Pow an Anethow
Alice in Cornish, 2009

La Aventuroj de Alicio en Mirlando
Alice in Esperanto, 2009

Les Aventures d'Alice au pays des merveilles
Alice in French, 2010

Alice's Abenteuer im Wunderland
Alice in German, 2010

Le Avventure di Alice nel Paese delle Meraviglie
Alice in Italian, 2010

Contoyrtyssyn Ealish ayns Çheer ny Yindyssyn
Alice in Manx, 2010

Alice's Äventyr i Sagolandet
Alice in Swedish, 2010

Anturiaethau Alys yng Ngwlad Hud
Alice in Welsh, 2010

CPSIA information can be obtained
at www.ICGtesting.com
Printed in the USA
LVIC05n1534200915
454953LV00001B/1

* 9 7 8 1 9 0 4 8 0 8 5 3 4 *